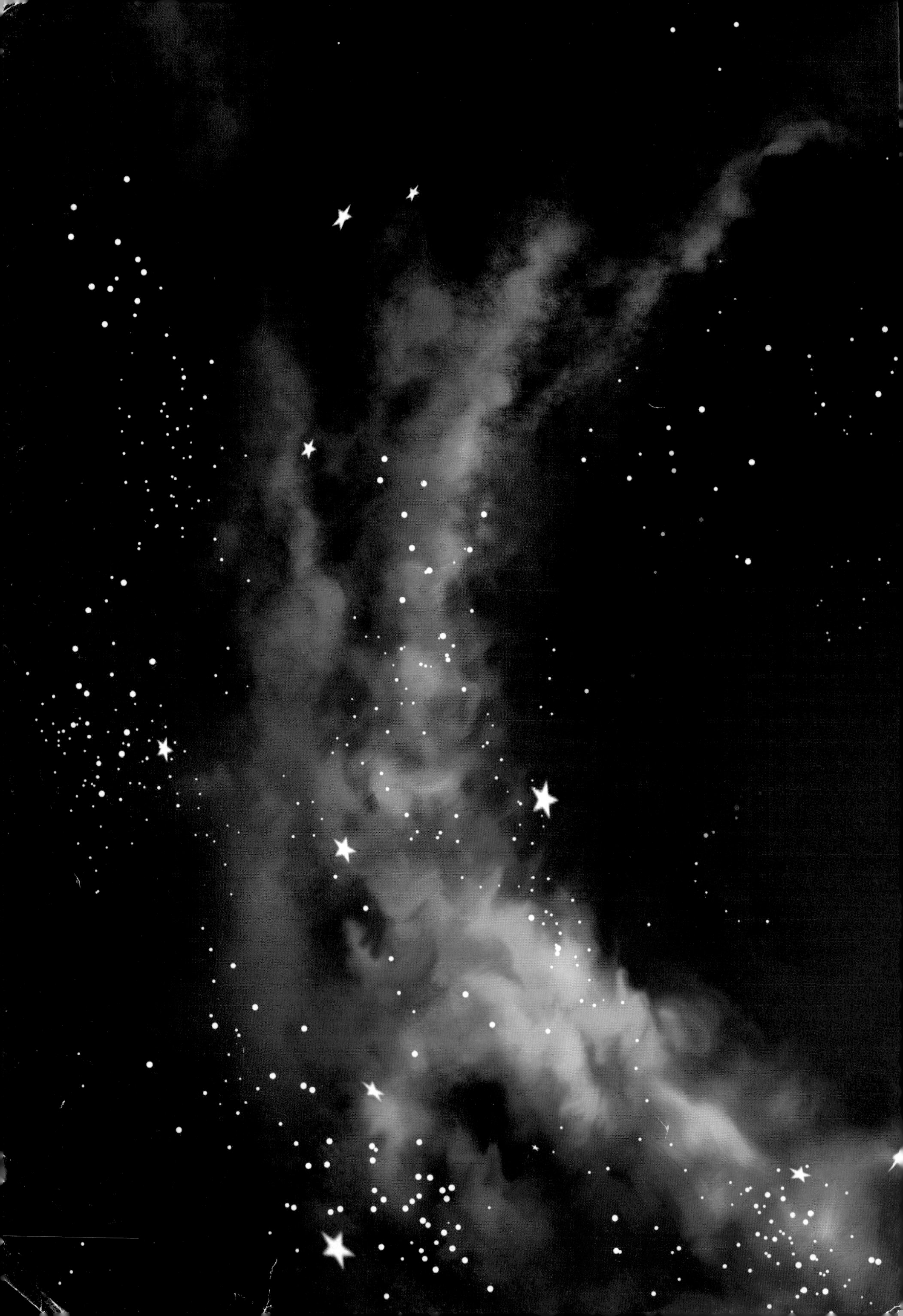

My dear Rose,

As we left the Planet of Gehom, I looked one last time at its unusual shape and marveled that no matter how different the planets we've landed on, the people we've met are basically the same.

The Cubists, like people everywhere, love freedom, yet most of them chose to follow a leader whose lust for power turned them into slaves in a never-ending quest for balance.

The Cubists found the courage to choose a different leader worthy of their trust and restore balance to their world.

Their victory gives me hope that the next people we meet can prevent their planet from turning against them and restore balance to their world.

The Little Prince

First American edition published in 2014 by Graphic Universe™.

Le Petit Prince®

based on the masterpiece by Antoine de Saint-Exupéry

Graphic Universe™
A division of Lerner Publishing Group, Inc.
241 First Avenue North
Minneapolis, MN 55401 USA

For reading levels and more information, look up this title at www.lernerbooks.com.

Library of Congress Cataloging-in-Publication Data
Dobel, Jean-Marc.
    [Planète du Bubble Gob. English]
    The Planet of the Bubble Gob / story by Jean-Marc Dobel ; design and illustrations by Elyum Studio ; adaptation by Clotilde Bruneau ; translation : Anne Collins Smith and Owen Smith. — First American edition.
        p.   cm. — (The little prince ; #17)
    ISBN 978-0-7613-8767-1 (lib. bdg. : alk. paper)
    ISBN 978-1-4677-4663-2 (eBook)
    1. Graphic novels. [1. Graphic novels.] I. Bruneau, Clotilde. II. Smith, Anne Collins, translator. III. Smith, Owen (Owen M.), translator. IV. Saint-Exupéry, Antoine de, 1900-1944. Petit prince. V. Elyum Studio. VI. Petit Prince (Television program) VII. Title.
    PZ7.7.D63Pl 2014
    741.5'944—de23   2013043588

Manufactured in the United States of America
1 — DP — 7/15/14

THE NEW ADVENTURES
BASED ON THE MASTERPIECE BY ANTOINE DE SAINT-EXUPÉRY

The Little Prince

THE PLANET OF THE BUBBLE GOB

Based on the animated series and an original story by Jean-Marc Dobel

Design: Elyum Studio
Story: Clotilde Bruneau
Artistic Direction: Didier Poli
Art: Diane Fayolle
Backgrounds: Isa Python
Coloring: Moonsun
Editing: Christine Chatal
Editorial Consultant: Didier Convard

Translation: Anne and Owen Smith

Graphic Universe™ • Minneapolis

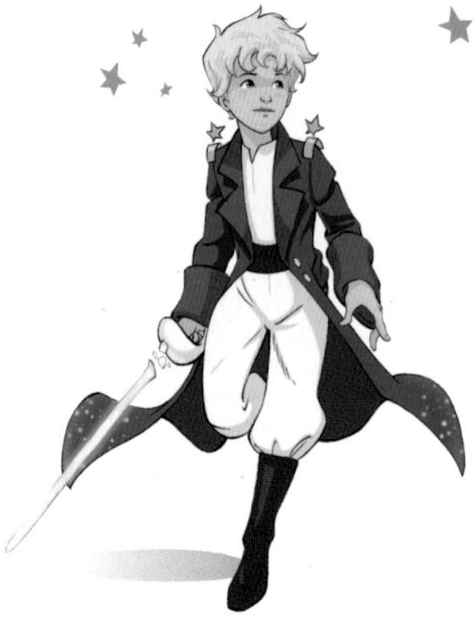

THE LITTLE PRINCE

The Little Prince has extraordinary gifts. His sense of wonder allows him to discover what no one else can see. The Little Prince can communicate with all the beings in the universe, even the animals and plants. His powers grow over the course of his adventures.

The Prince's uniform:
When he transforms into the uniform of a prince, he is more agile and quick. When faced with difficult situations, the Little Prince also uses a sword that lets him sketch and bring to life anything from his imagination.

His sketchbook:
When he is not in his Prince's clothing, the Little Prince carries a sketchbook. When he blows on the pages, they take wing and form objects that he'll find very useful. Like his sword, it's powered by stardust collected on his travels.

FOX

A grouch, a trickster, and, so he says, interested only in his next meal, Fox is in reality the Little Prince's best friend. As such, he is always there to give him help but also just as much to help him to grow and to learn about the world.

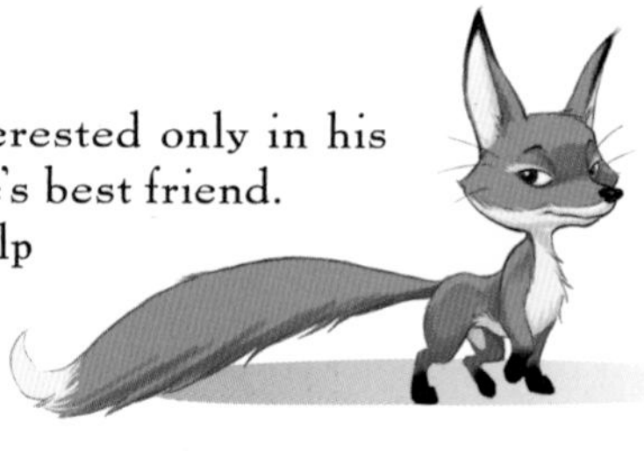

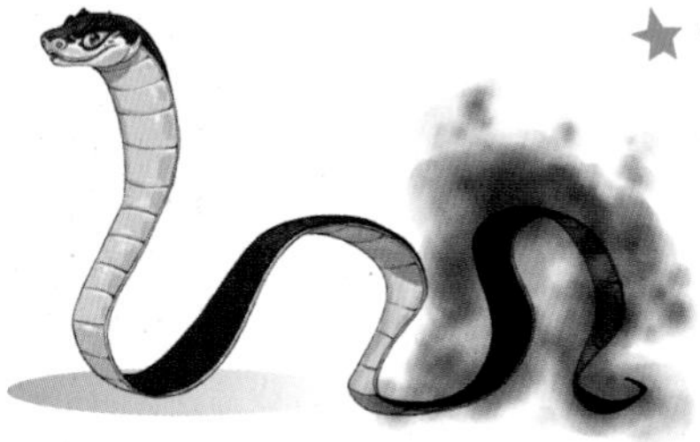

THE SNAKE

Even though the Little Prince still does not know exactly why, there can be no doubt that the Snake has set his mind to plunging the entire universe into darkness! And to accomplish his goal, this malicious being is ready to use any form of deception. However, the Snake never takes action himself. He prefers to bring out the wickedness in those beings he has chosen to bite, tempting them to put their own worlds in danger.

THE GLOOMIES

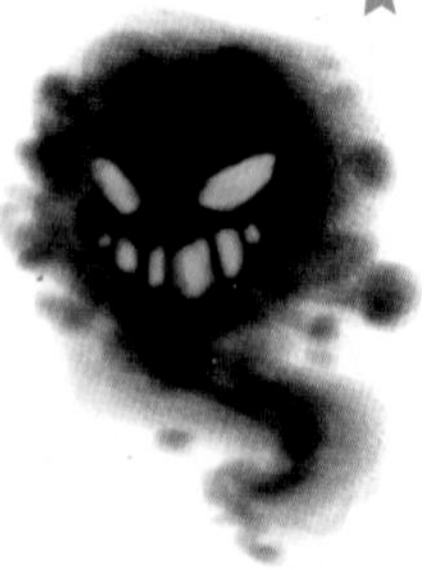

When people who have been "bitten" by the Snake have completely destroyed their own planets, they become Gloomies, slaves to their Snake master. The Gloomies act as a group and carry out the Snake's most vile orders so he can get the better of the Little Prince!

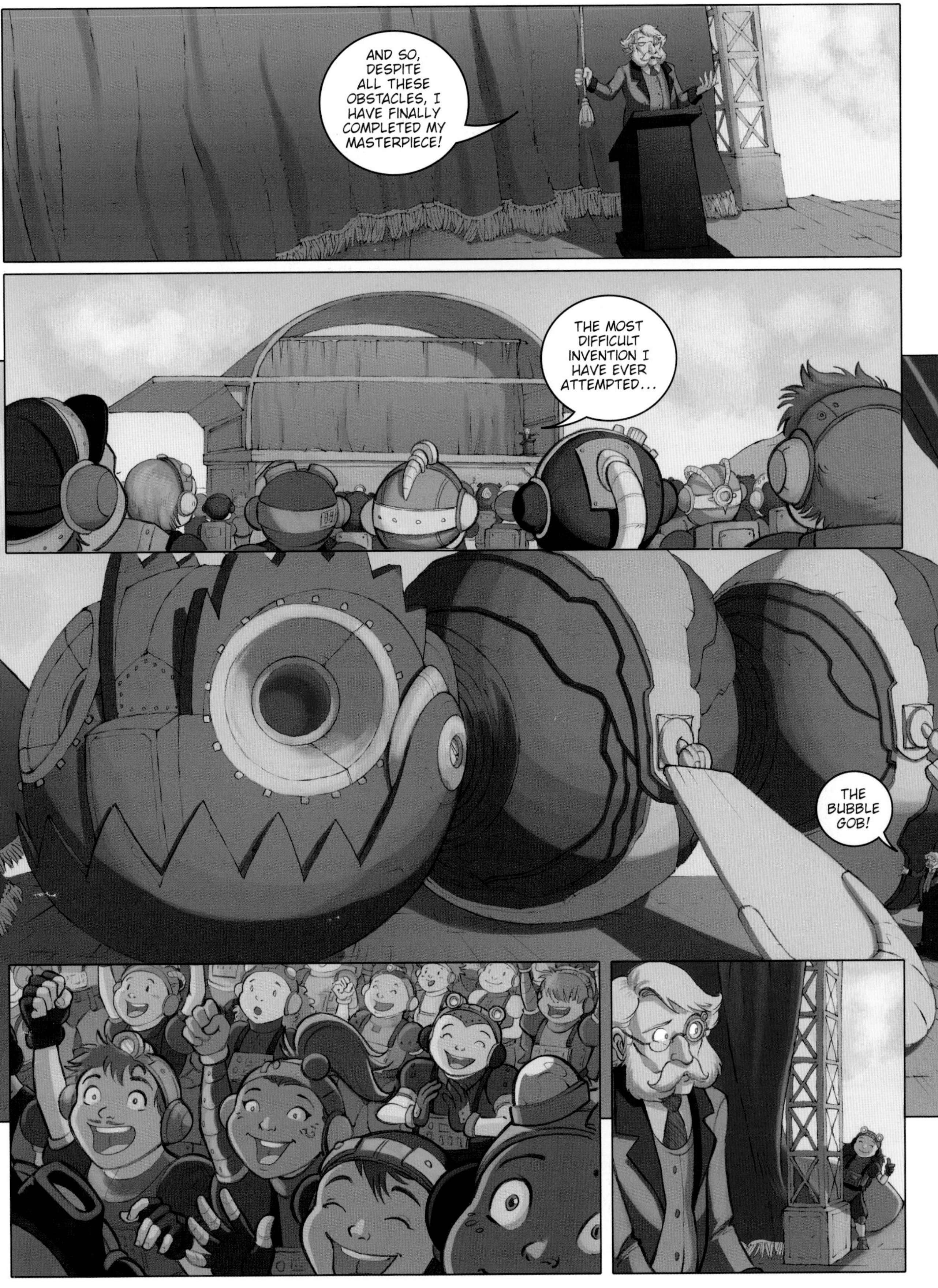
AND SO, DESPITE ALL THESE OBSTACLES, I HAVE FINALLY COMPLETED MY MASTERPIECE!
THE MOST DIFFICULT INVENTION I HAVE EVER ATTEMPTED...
THE BUBBLE GOB!

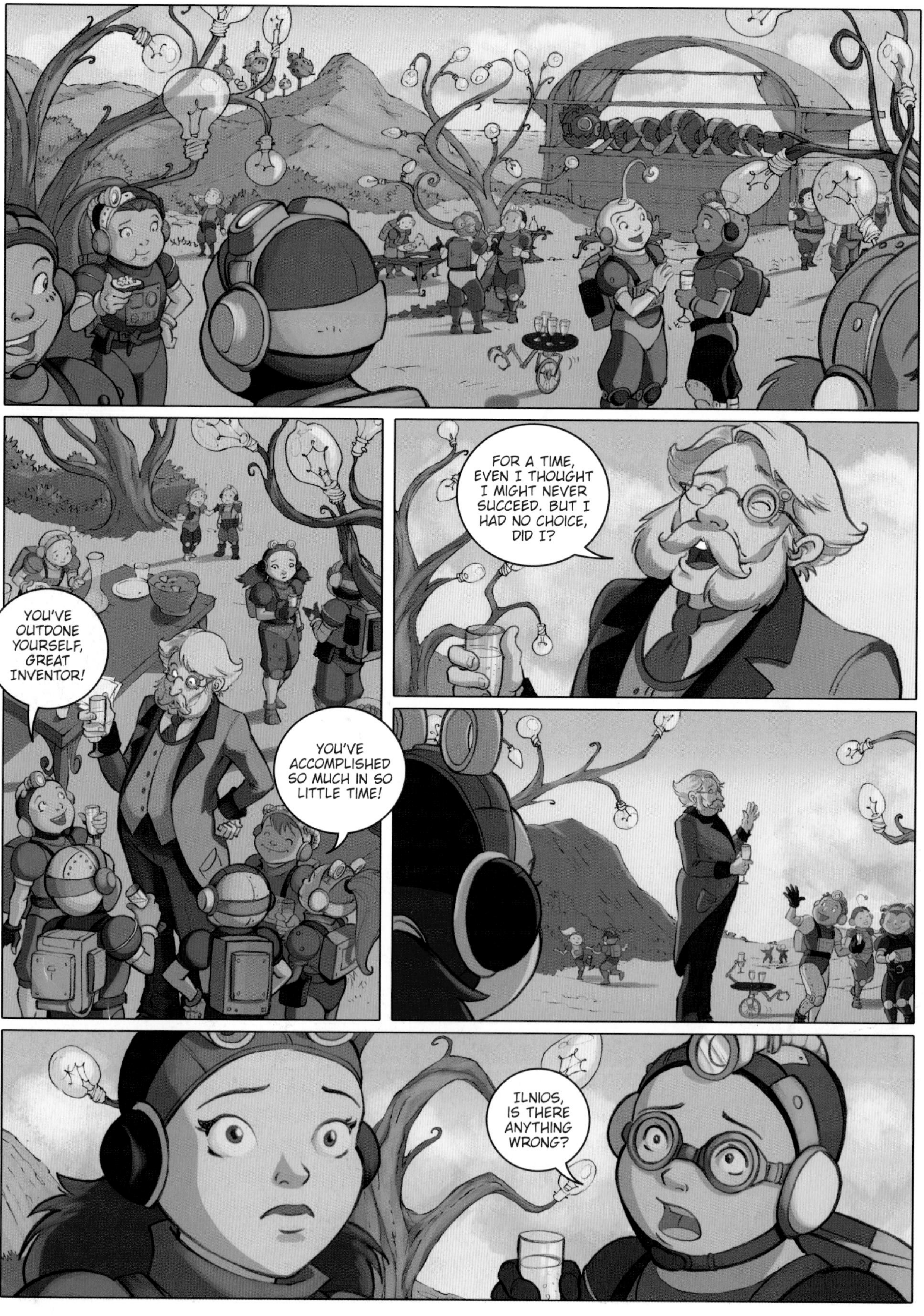

YOU'VE OUTDONE YOURSELF, GREAT INVENTOR!
YOU'VE ACCOMPLISHED SO MUCH IN SO LITTLE TIME!
FOR A TIME, EVEN I THOUGHT I MIGHT NEVER SUCCEED. BUT I HAD NO CHOICE, DID I?
ILNIOS, IS THERE ANYTHING WRONG?

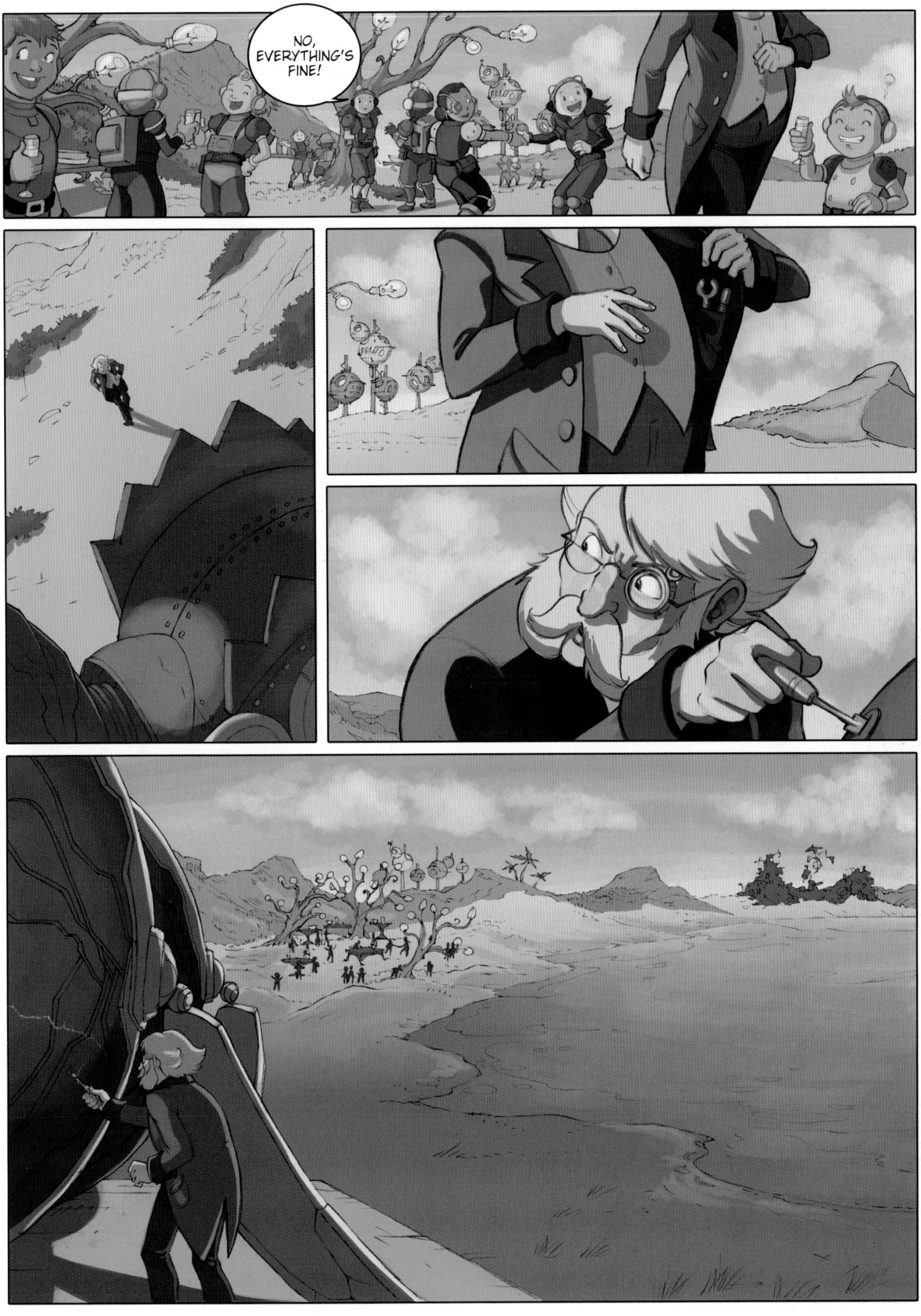
NO, EVERYTHING'S FINE!

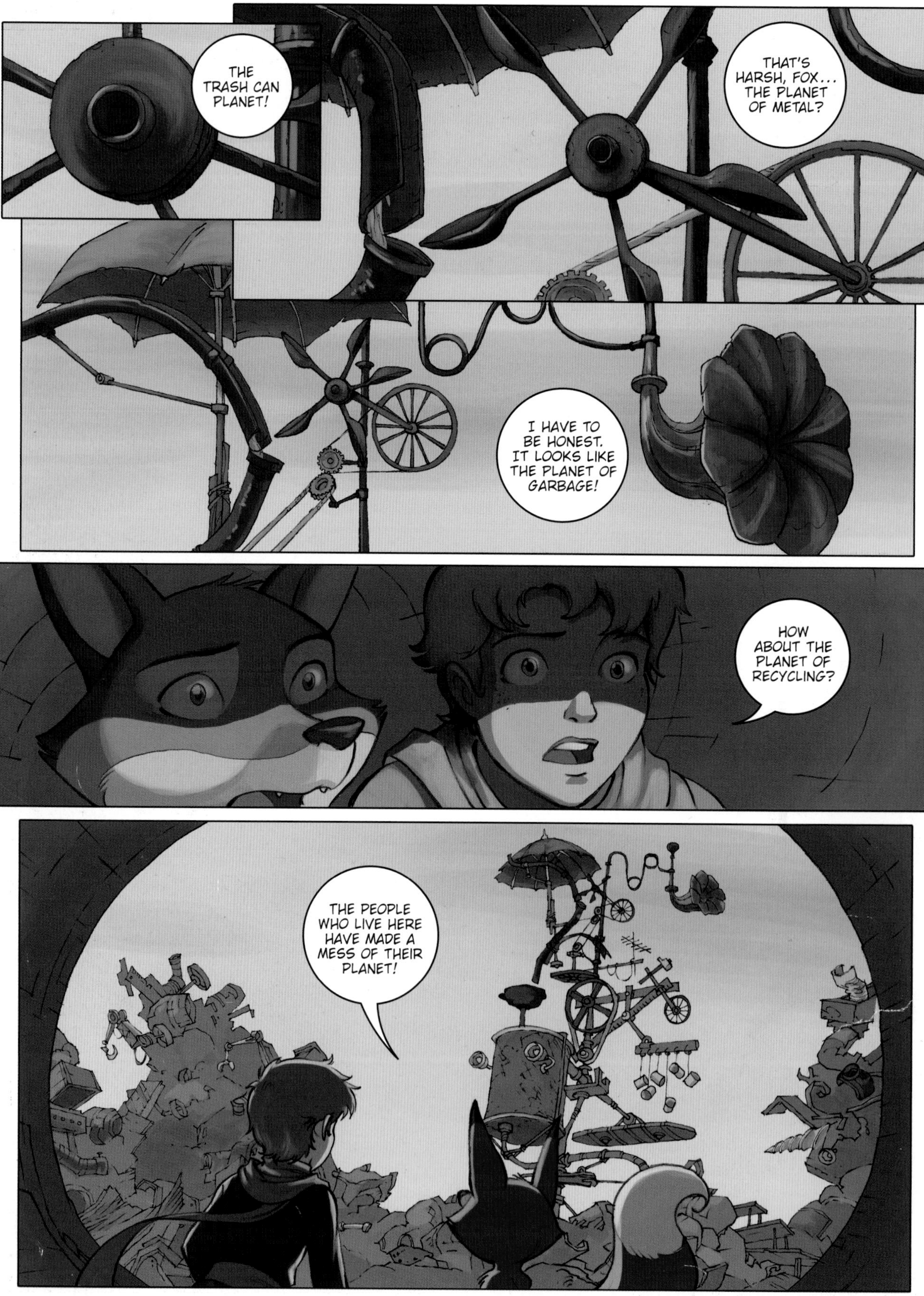
THE TRASH CAN PLANET!
THAT'S HARSH, FOX... THE PLANET OF METAL?
I HAVE TO BE HONEST. IT LOOKS LIKE THE PLANET OF GARBAGE!
HOW ABOUT THE PLANET OF RECYCLING?
THE PEOPLE WHO LIVE HERE HAVE MADE A MESS OF THEIR PLANET!

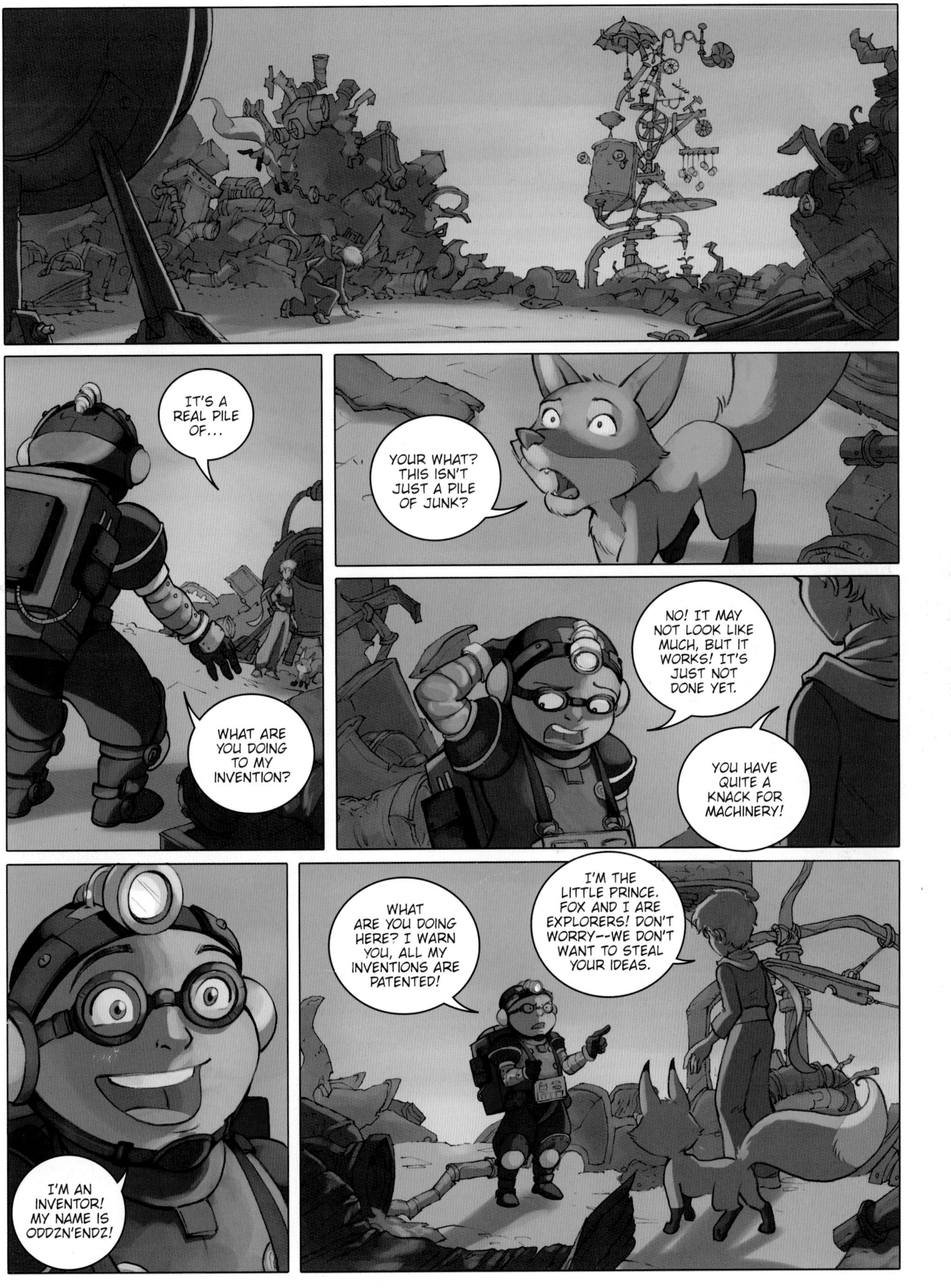
IT'S A REAL PILE OF...
YOUR WHAT? THIS ISN'T JUST A PILE OF JUNK?
WHAT ARE YOU DOING TO MY INVENTION?
NO! IT MAY NOT LOOK LIKE MUCH, BUT IT WORKS! IT'S JUST NOT DONE YET.
YOU HAVE QUITE A KNACK FOR MACHINERY!
I'M AN INVENTOR! MY NAME IS ODDZN'ENDZ!
WHAT ARE YOU DOING HERE? I WARN YOU, ALL MY INVENTIONS ARE PATENTED!
I'M THE LITTLE PRINCE. FOX AND I ARE EXPLORERS! DON'T WORRY--WE DON'T WANT TO STEAL YOUR IDEAS.

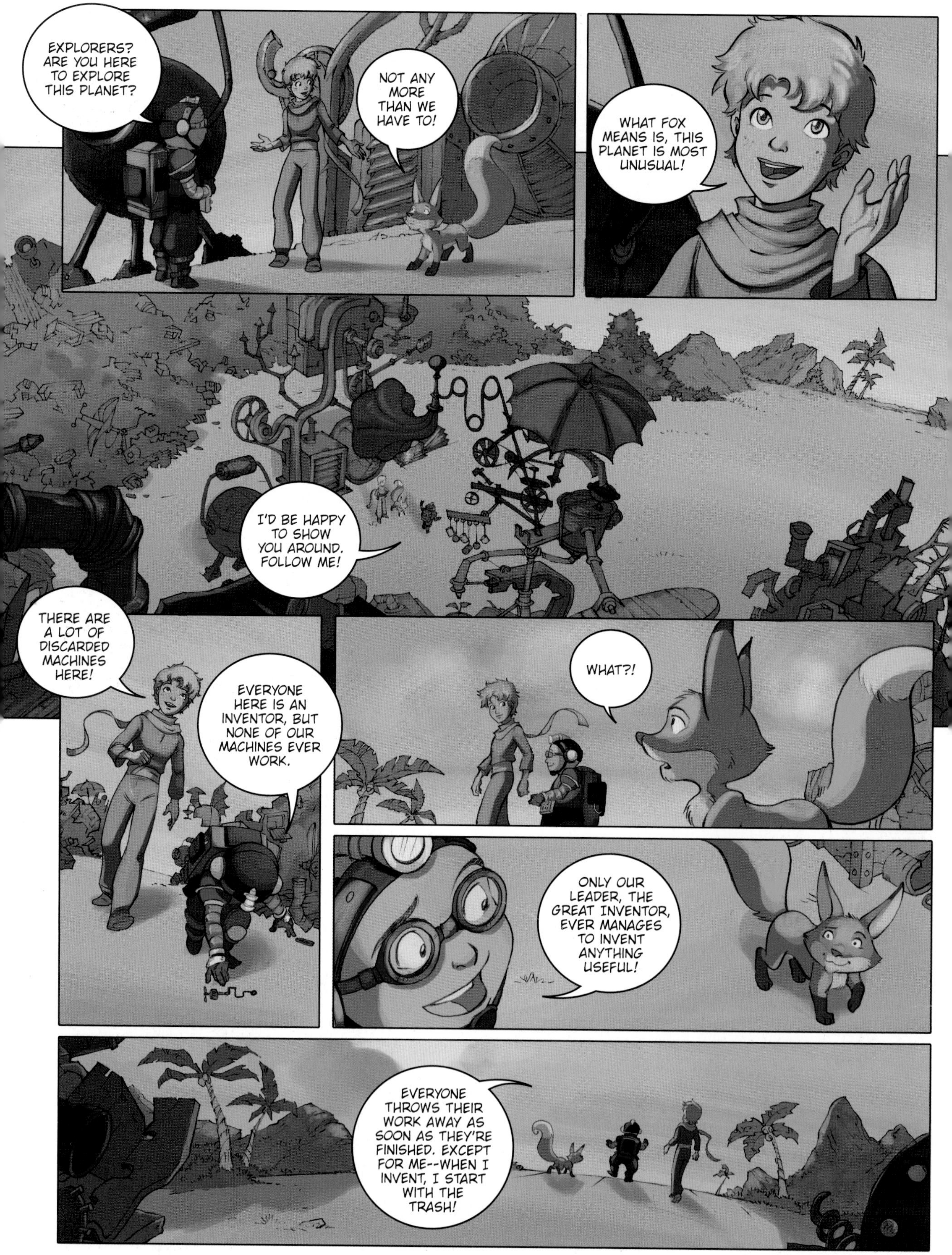
EXPLORERS? ARE YOU HERE TO EXPLORE THIS PLANET?
NOT ANY MORE THAN WE HAVE TO!
WHAT FOX MEANS IS, THIS PLANET IS MOST UNUSUAL!
I'D BE HAPPY TO SHOW YOU AROUND. FOLLOW ME!
THERE ARE A LOT OF DISCARDED MACHINES HERE!
EVERYONE HERE IS AN INVENTOR, BUT NONE OF OUR MACHINES EVER WORK.
WHAT?!
ONLY OUR LEADER, THE GREAT INVENTOR, EVER MANAGES TO INVENT ANYTHING USEFUL!
EVERYONE THROWS THEIR WORK AWAY AS SOON AS THEY'RE FINISHED. EXCEPT FOR ME--WHEN I INVENT, I START WITH THE TRASH!

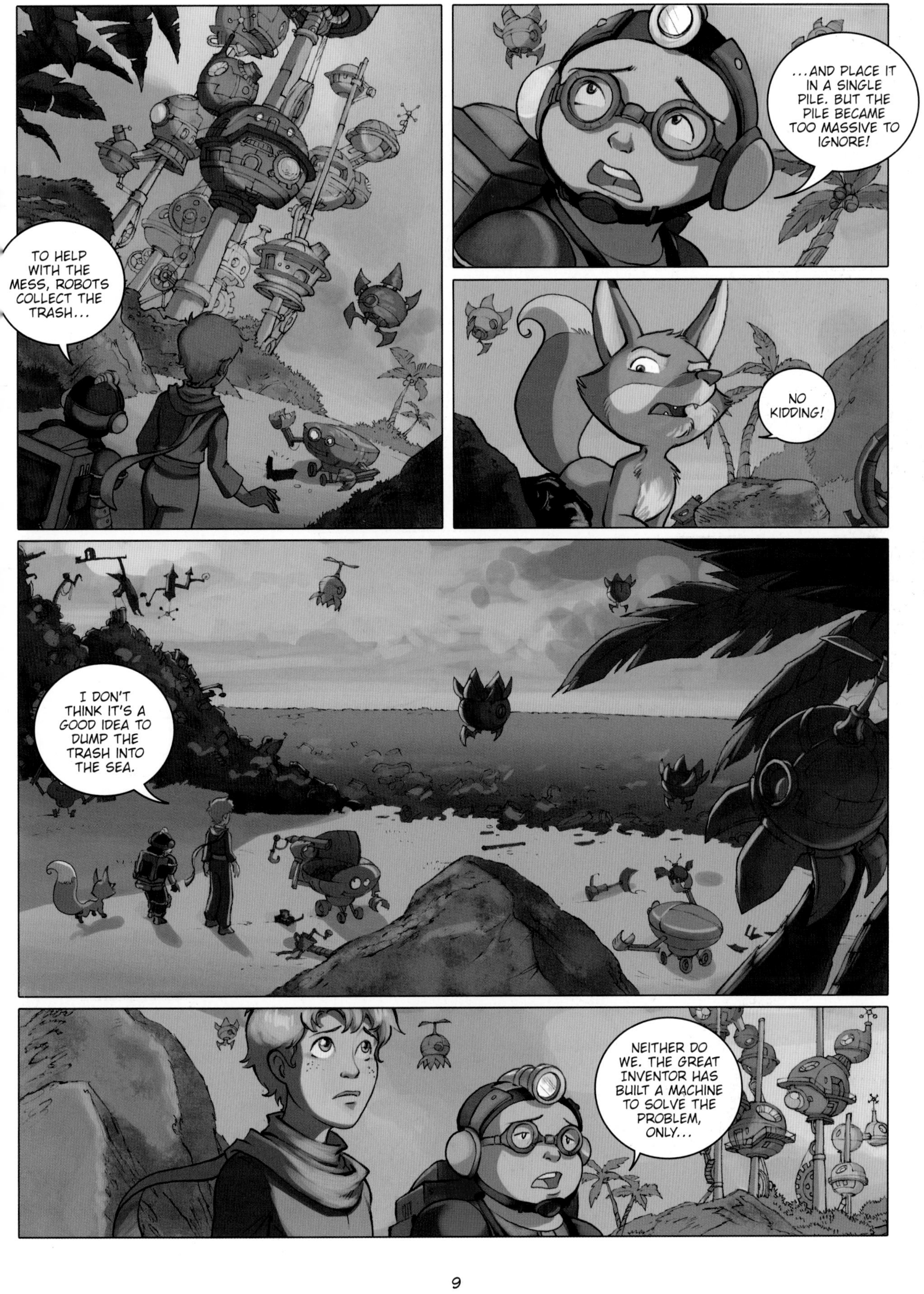
TO HELP WITH THE MESS, ROBOTS COLLECT THE TRASH...
...AND PLACE IT IN A SINGLE PILE. BUT THE PILE BECAME TOO MASSIVE TO IGNORE!
NO KIDDING!
I DON'T THINK IT'S A GOOD IDEA TO DUMP THE TRASH INTO THE SEA.
NEITHER DO WE. THE GREAT INVENTOR HAS BUILT A MACHINE TO SOLVE THE PROBLEM, ONLY...

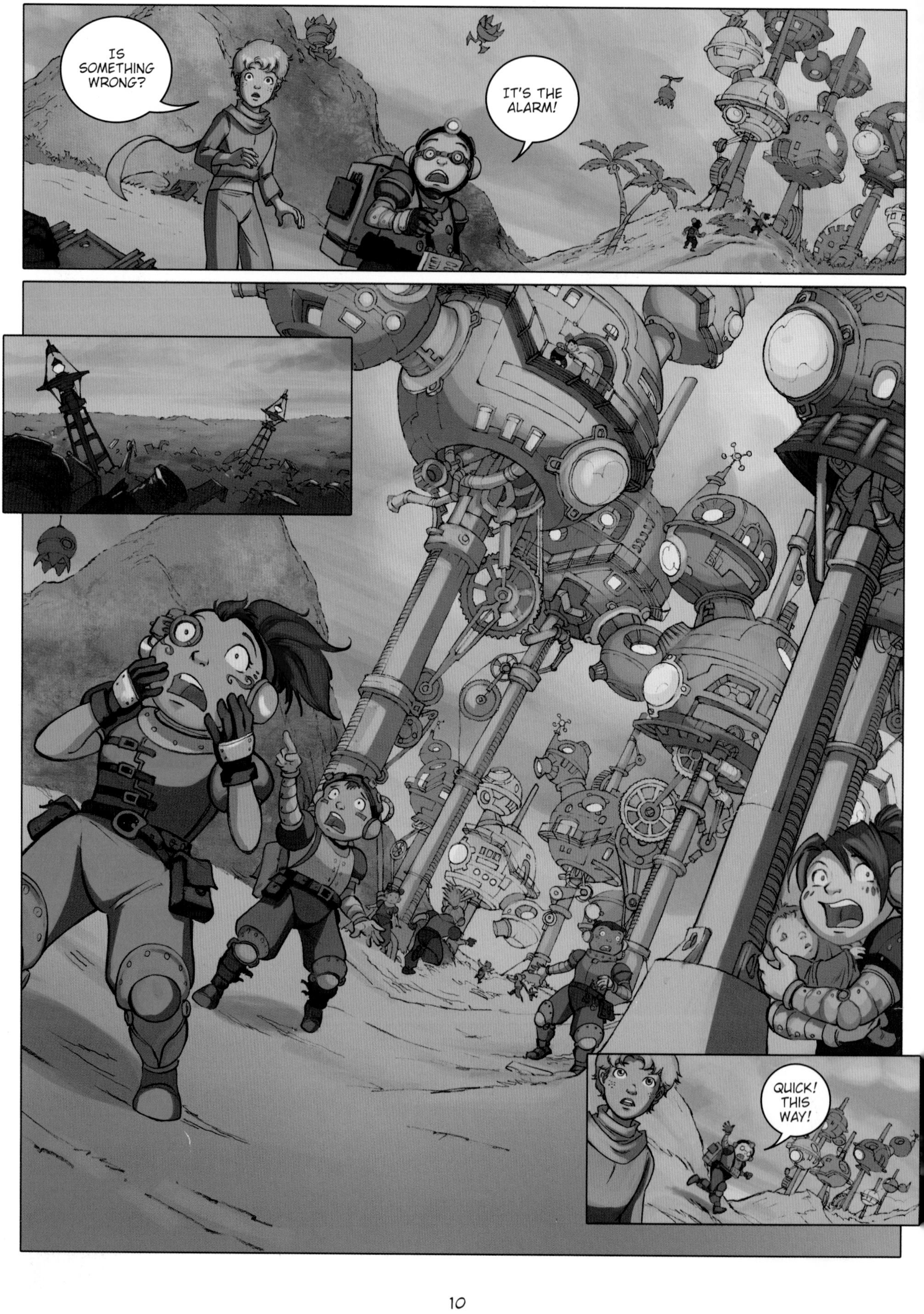
IS SOMETHING WRONG?
IT'S THE ALARM!
QUICK! THIS WAY!

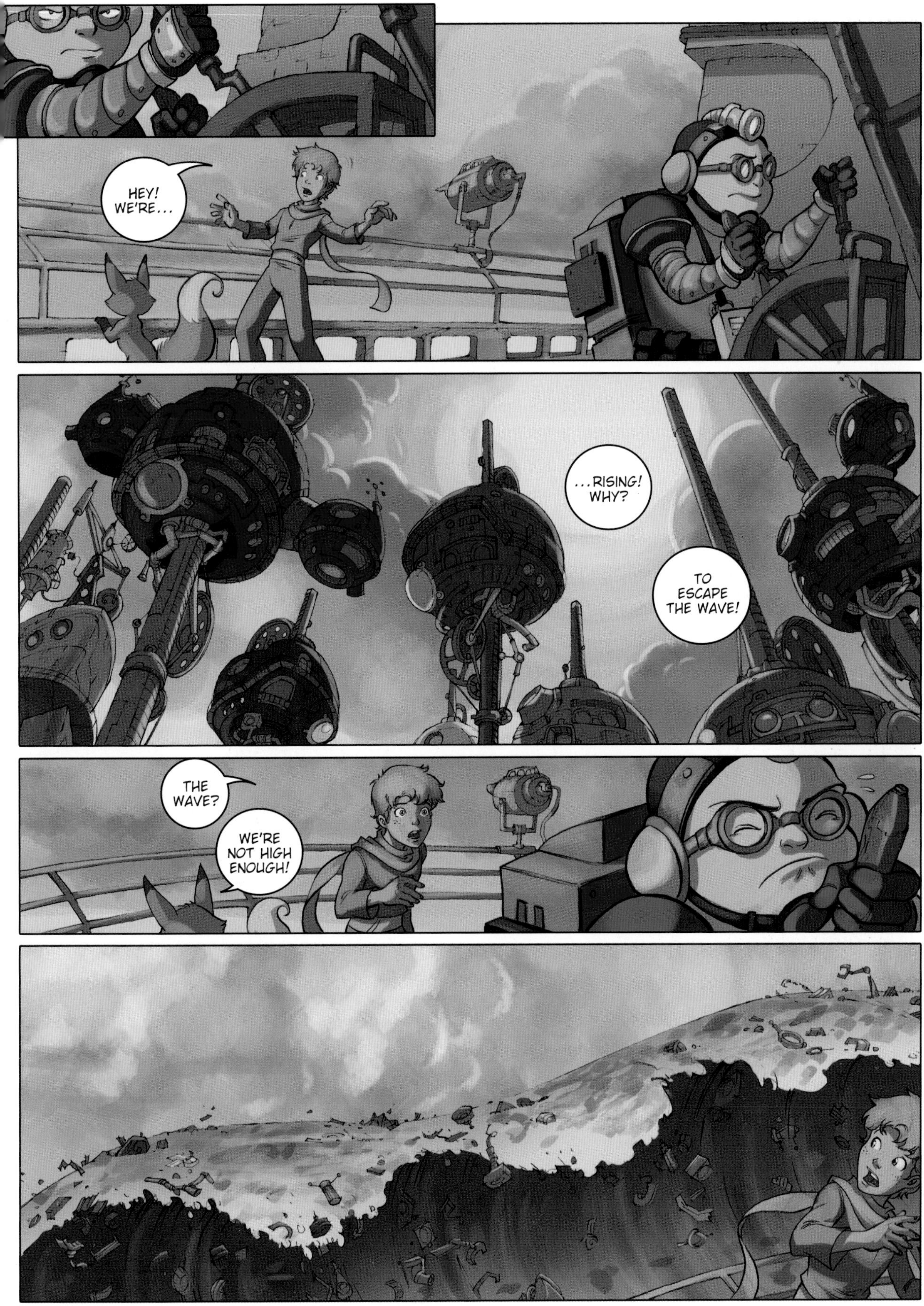
HEY! WE'RE...
...RISING! WHY?
TO ESCAPE THE WAVE!
THE WAVE?
WE'RE NOT HIGH ENOUGH!

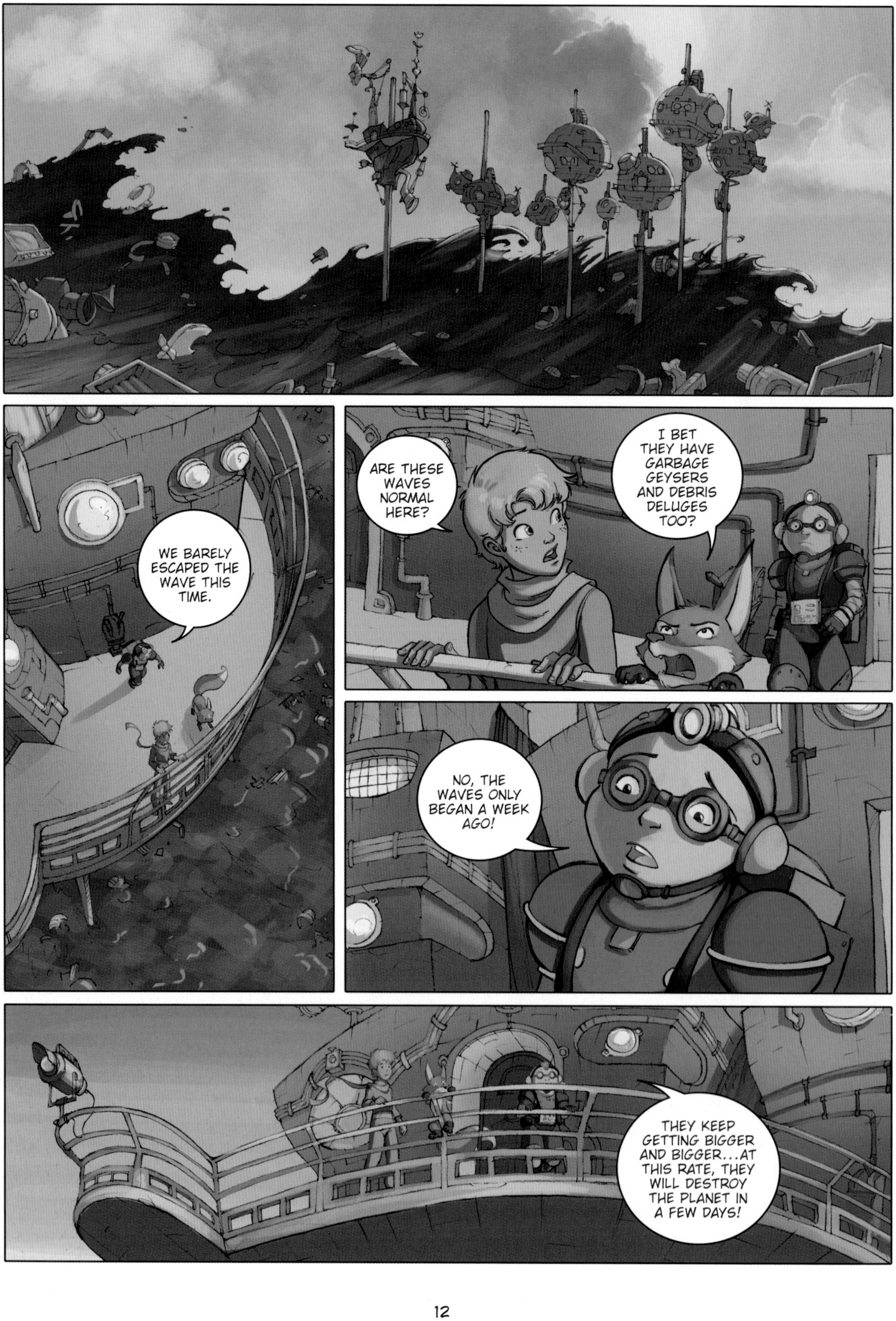
WE BARELY ESCAPED THE WAVE THIS TIME.
ARE THESE WAVES NORMAL HERE?
I BET THEY HAVE GARBAGE GEYSERS AND DEBRIS DELUGES TOO?
NO, THE WAVES ONLY BEGAN A WEEK AGO!
THEY KEEP GETTING BIGGER AND BIGGER...AT THIS RATE, THEY WILL DESTROY THE PLANET IN A FEW DAYS!

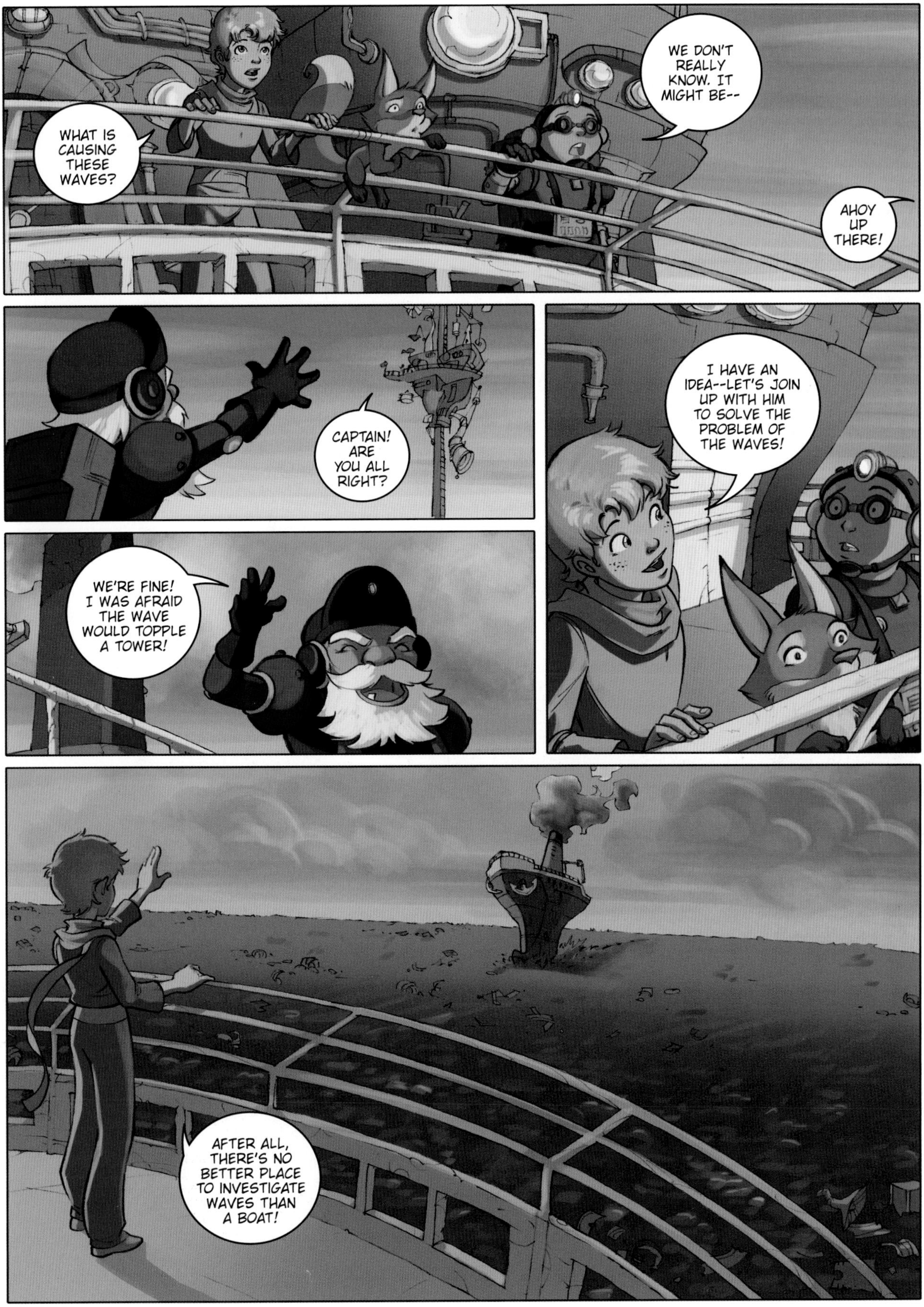

WHAT IS CAUSING THESE WAVES?
WE DON'T REALLY KNOW. IT MIGHT BE--
AHOY UP THERE!
CAPTAIN! ARE YOU ALL RIGHT?
WE'RE FINE! I WAS AFRAID THE WAVE WOULD TOPPLE A TOWER!
I HAVE AN IDEA--LET'S JOIN UP WITH HIM TO SOLVE THE PROBLEM OF THE WAVES!
AFTER ALL, THERE'S NO BETTER PLACE TO INVESTIGATE WAVES THAN A BOAT!

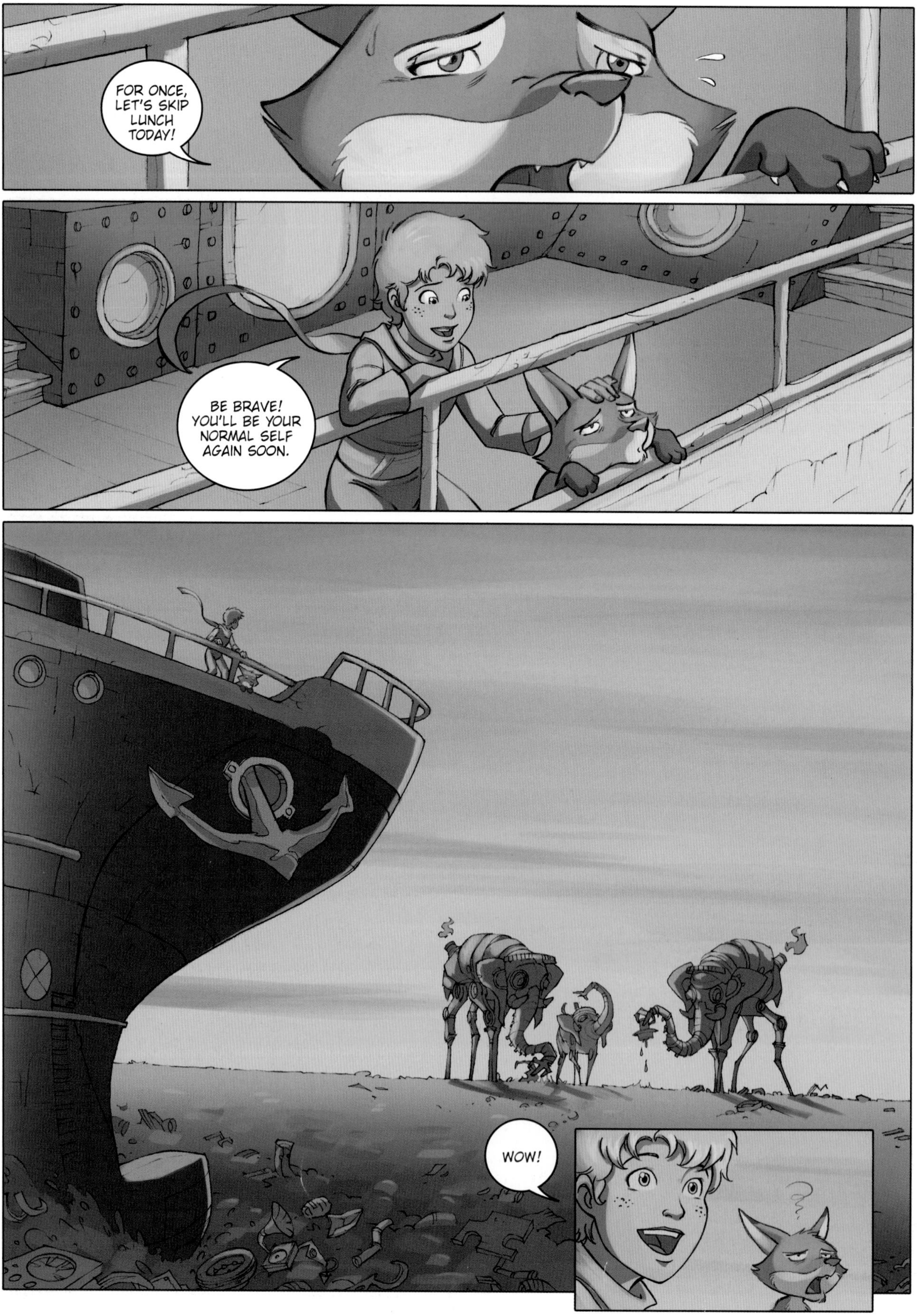
FOR ONCE, LET'S SKIP LUNCH TODAY!
BE BRAVE! YOU'LL BE YOUR NORMAL SELF AGAIN SOON.
WOW!

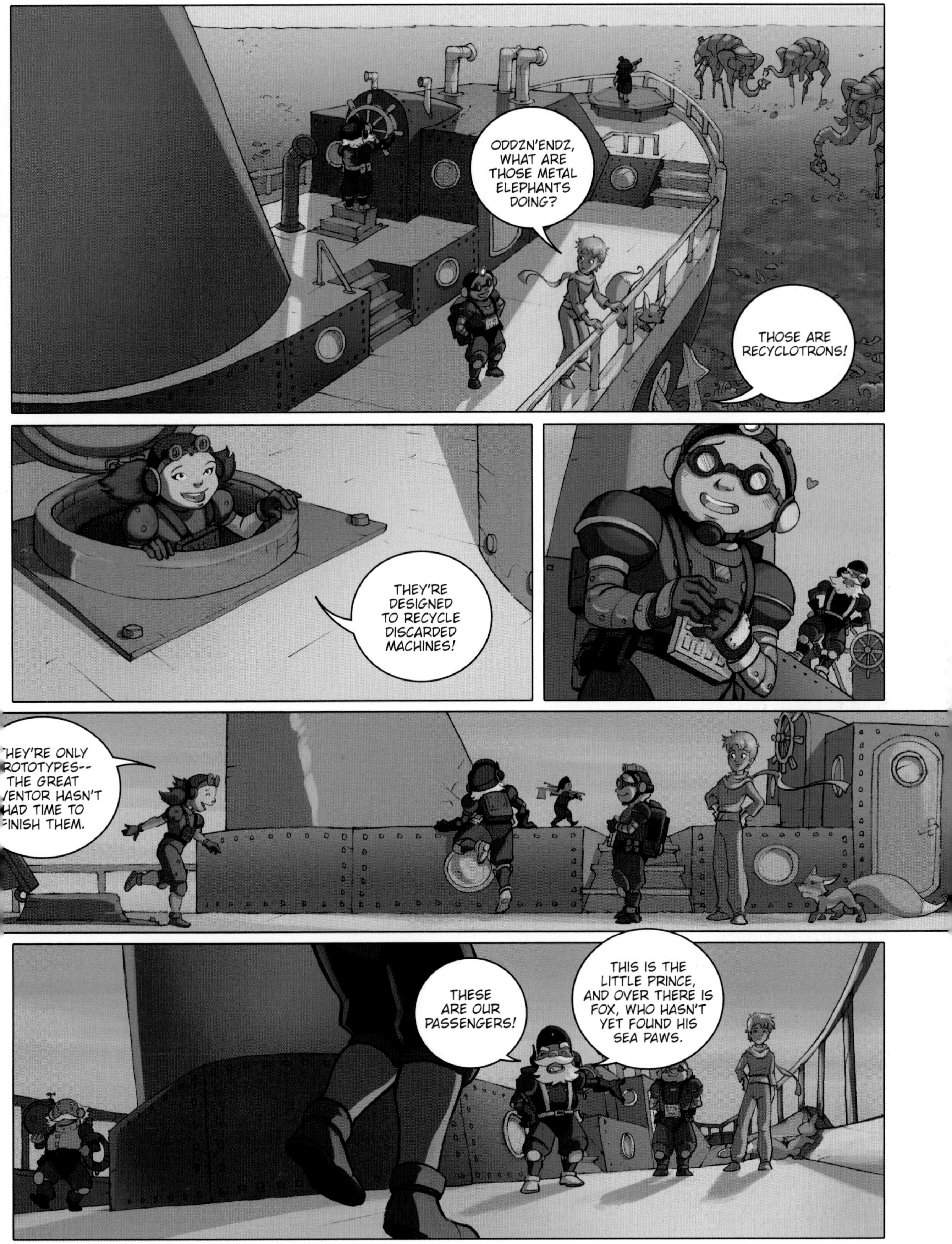
ODDZN'ENDZ, WHAT ARE THOSE METAL ELEPHANTS DOING?
THOSE ARE RECYCLOTRONS!
THEY'RE DESIGNED TO RECYCLE DISCARDED MACHINES!
THEY'RE ONLY PROTOTYPES-- THE GREAT INVENTOR HASN'T HAD TIME TO FINISH THEM.
THESE ARE OUR PASSENGERS!
THIS IS THE LITTLE PRINCE, AND OVER THERE IS FOX, WHO HASN'T YET FOUND HIS SEA PAWS.

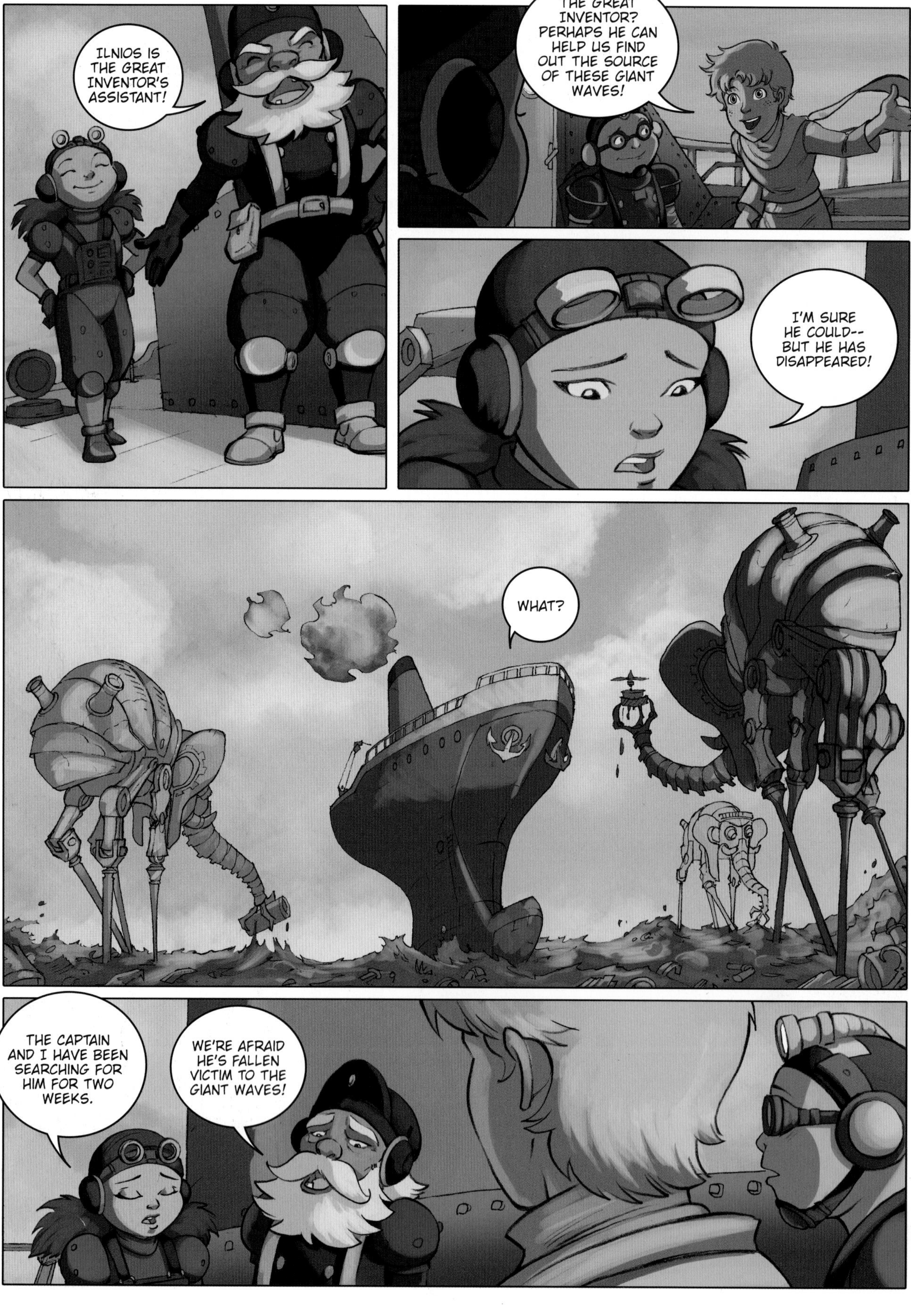
ILNIOS IS THE GREAT INVENTOR'S ASSISTANT!
THE GREAT INVENTOR? PERHAPS HE CAN HELP US FIND OUT THE SOURCE OF THESE GIANT WAVES!
I'M SURE HE COULD-- BUT HE HAS DISAPPEARED!
WHAT?
THE CAPTAIN AND I HAVE BEEN SEARCHING FOR HIM FOR TWO WEEKS.
WE'RE AFRAID HE'S FALLEN VICTIM TO THE GIANT WAVES!

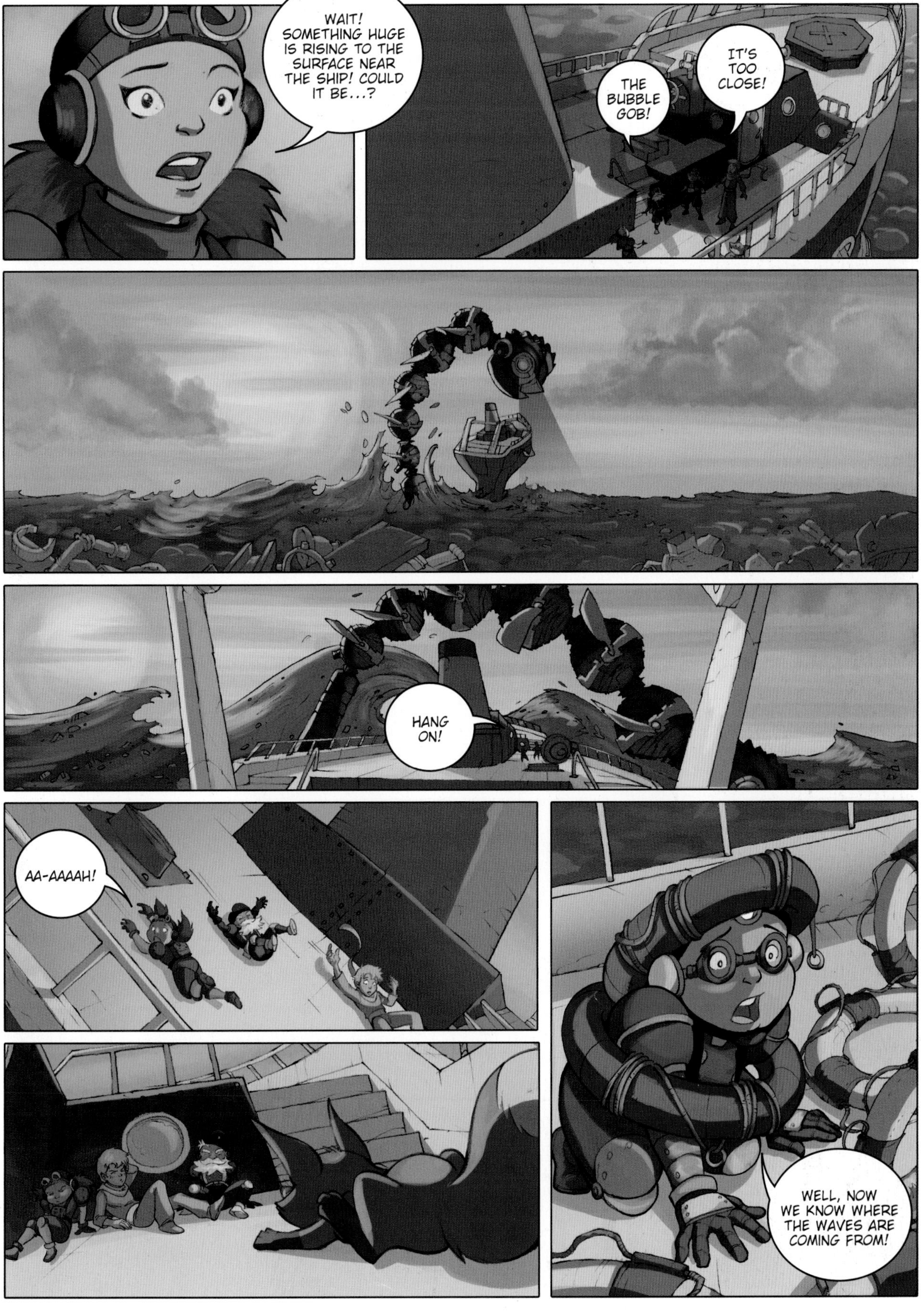
WAIT! SOMETHING HUGE IS RISING TO THE SURFACE NEAR THE SHIP! COULD IT BE...?
THE BUBBLE GOB!
IT'S TOO CLOSE!
HANG ON!
AA-AAAAH!
WELL, NOW WE KNOW WHERE THE WAVES ARE COMING FROM!

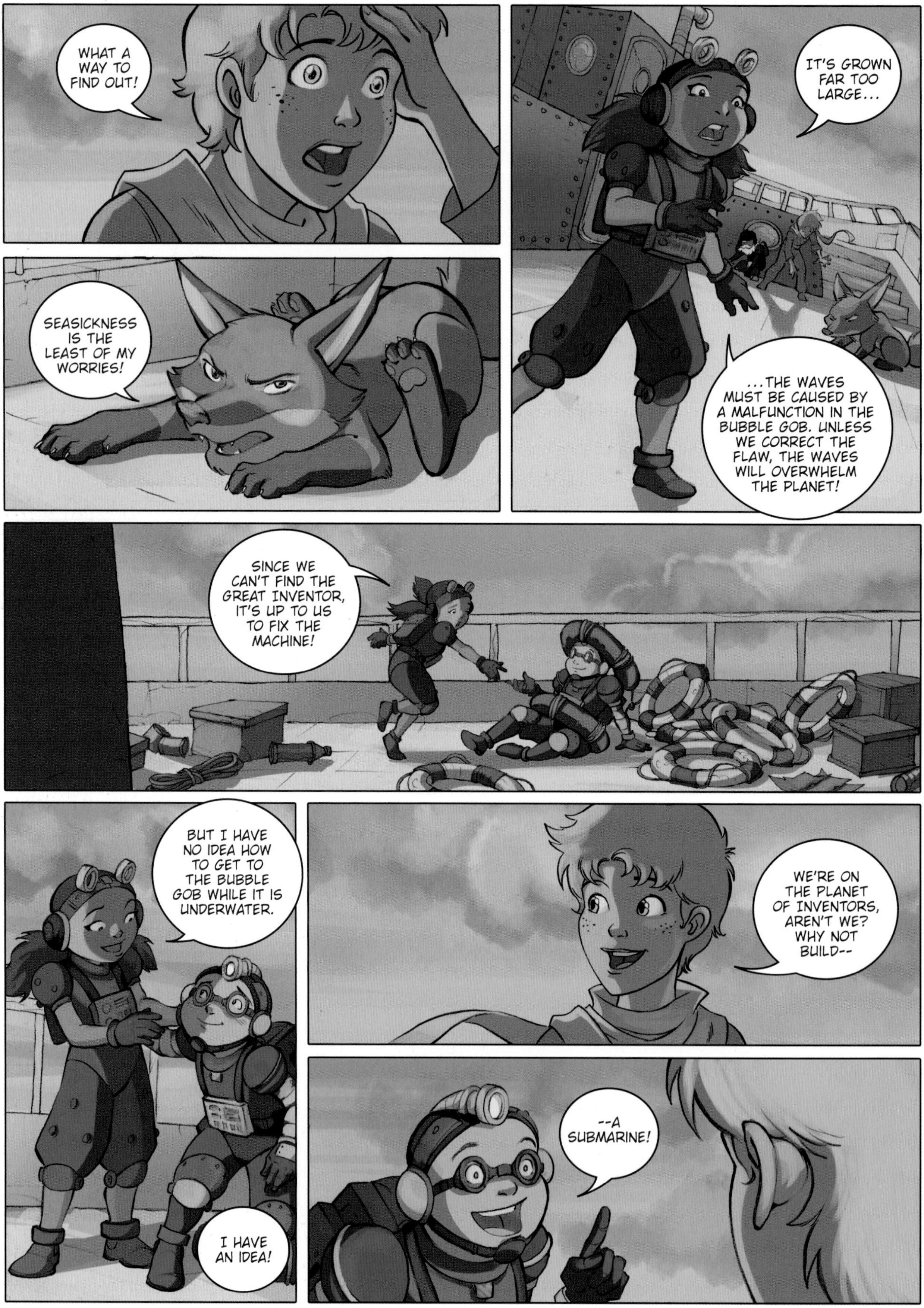
WHAT A WAY TO FIND OUT!
IT'S GROWN FAR TOO LARGE...
SEASICKNESS IS THE LEAST OF MY WORRIES!
...THE WAVES MUST BE CAUSED BY A MALFUNCTION IN THE BUBBLE GOB. UNLESS WE CORRECT THE FLAW, THE WAVES WILL OVERWHELM THE PLANET!
SINCE WE CAN'T FIND THE GREAT INVENTOR, IT'S UP TO US TO FIX THE MACHINE!
BUT I HAVE NO IDEA HOW TO GET TO THE BUBBLE GOB WHILE IT IS UNDERWATER.
I HAVE AN IDEA!
WE'RE ON THE PLANET OF INVENTORS, AREN'T WE? WHY NOT BUILD--
--A SUBMARINE!

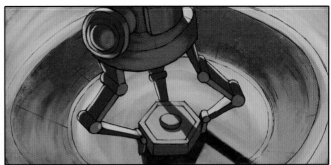
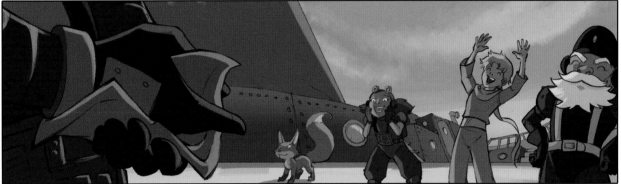

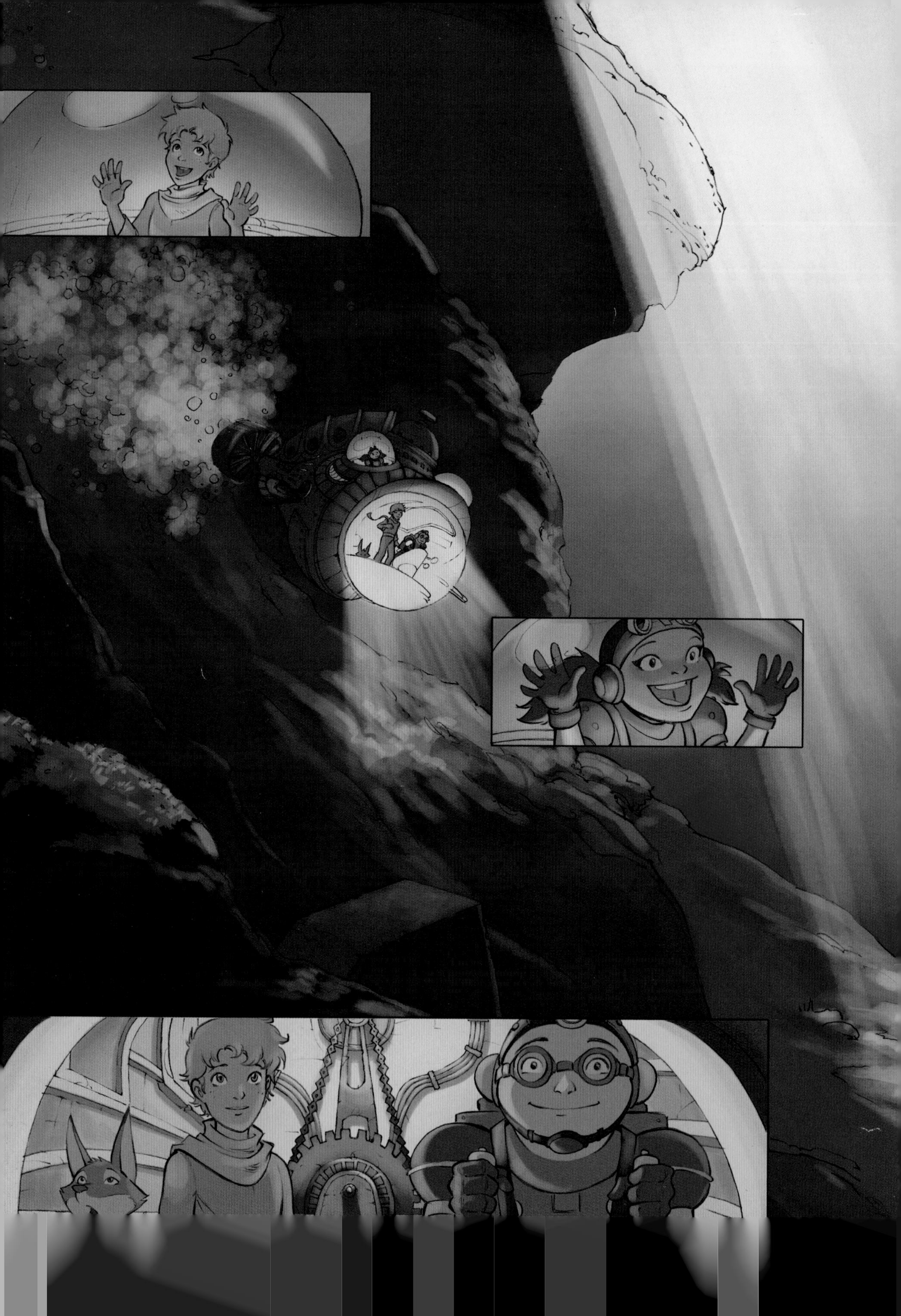

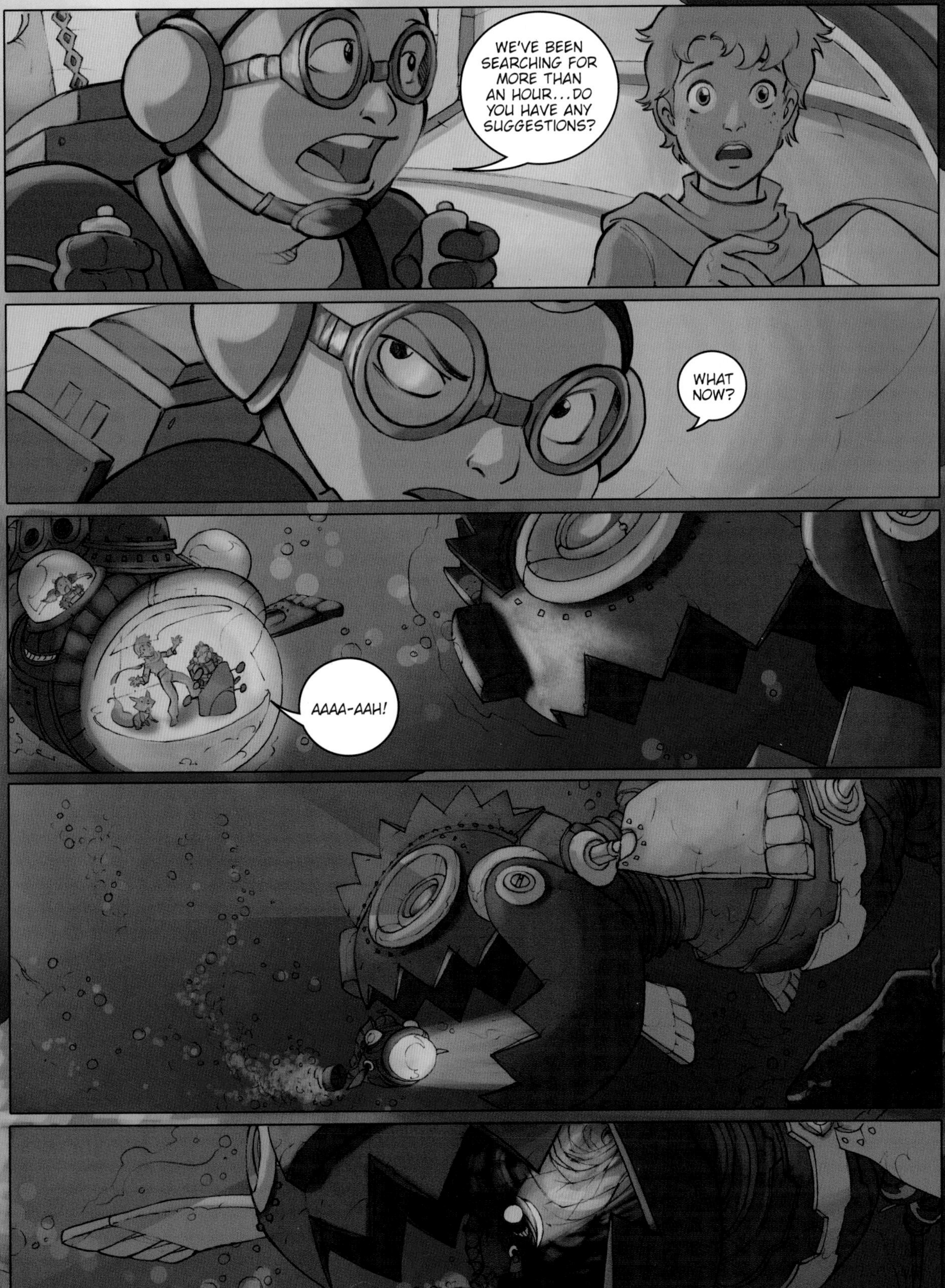
WE'VE BEEN SEARCHING FOR MORE THAN AN HOUR...DO YOU HAVE ANY SUGGESTIONS?
WHAT NOW?
AAAA-AAH!

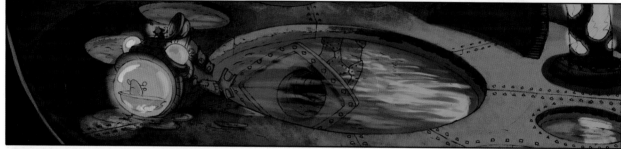

I KNOW WHERE WE ARE... EVERYTHING SEEMS TO BE WORKING CORRECTLY HERE!

WE'RE GOING TO HAVE TO EXPLORE THE BUBBLE GOB ON FOOT!

HOW DO WE FIND THE MALFUNCTION?

FOLLOW ME!

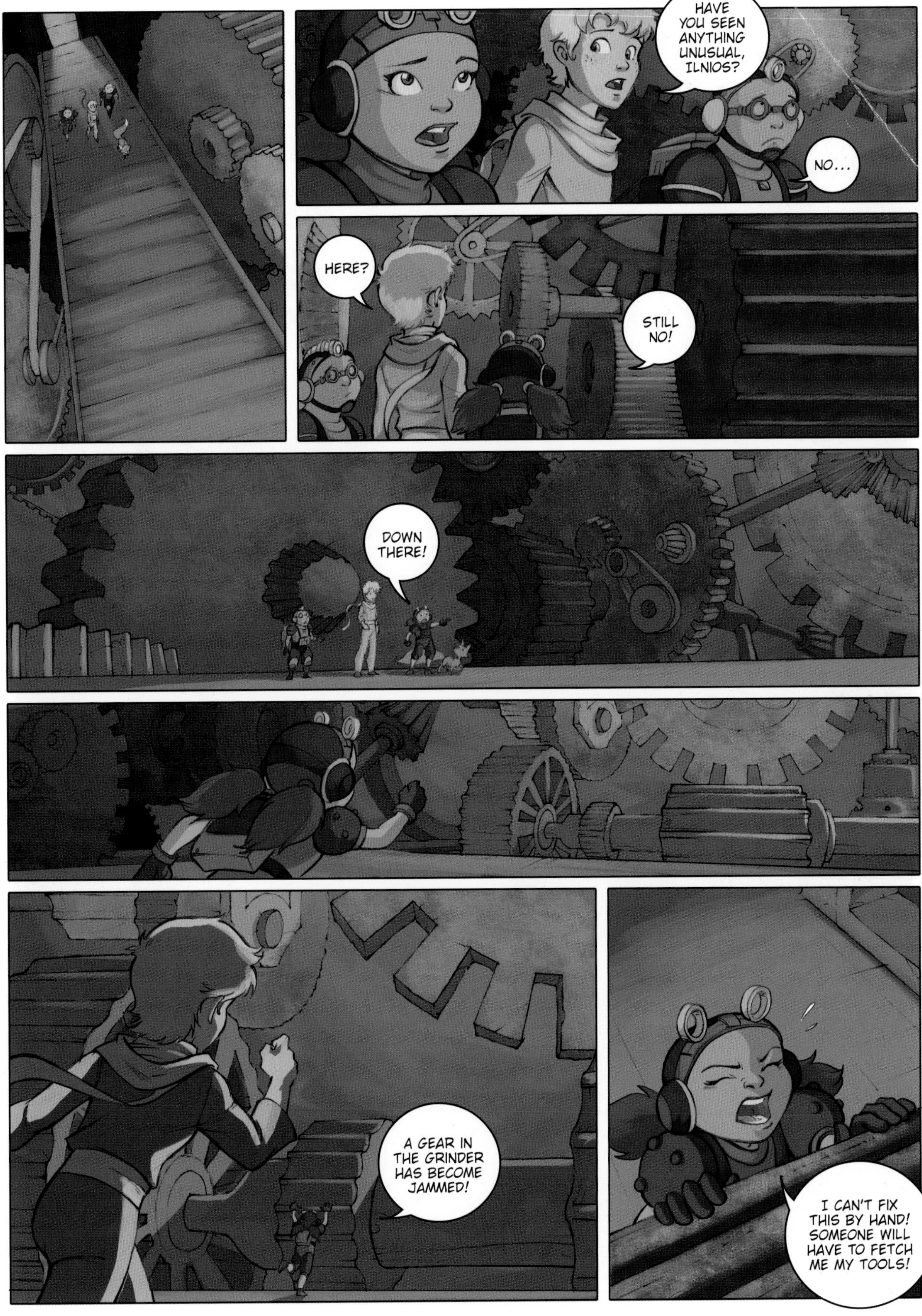
HAVE YOU SEEN ANYTHING UNUSUAL, ILNIOS?
NO...
HERE?
STILL NO!
DOWN THERE!
A GEAR IN THE GRINDER HAS BECOME JAMMED!
I CAN'T FIX THIS BY HAND! SOMEONE WILL HAVE TO FETCH ME MY TOOLS!

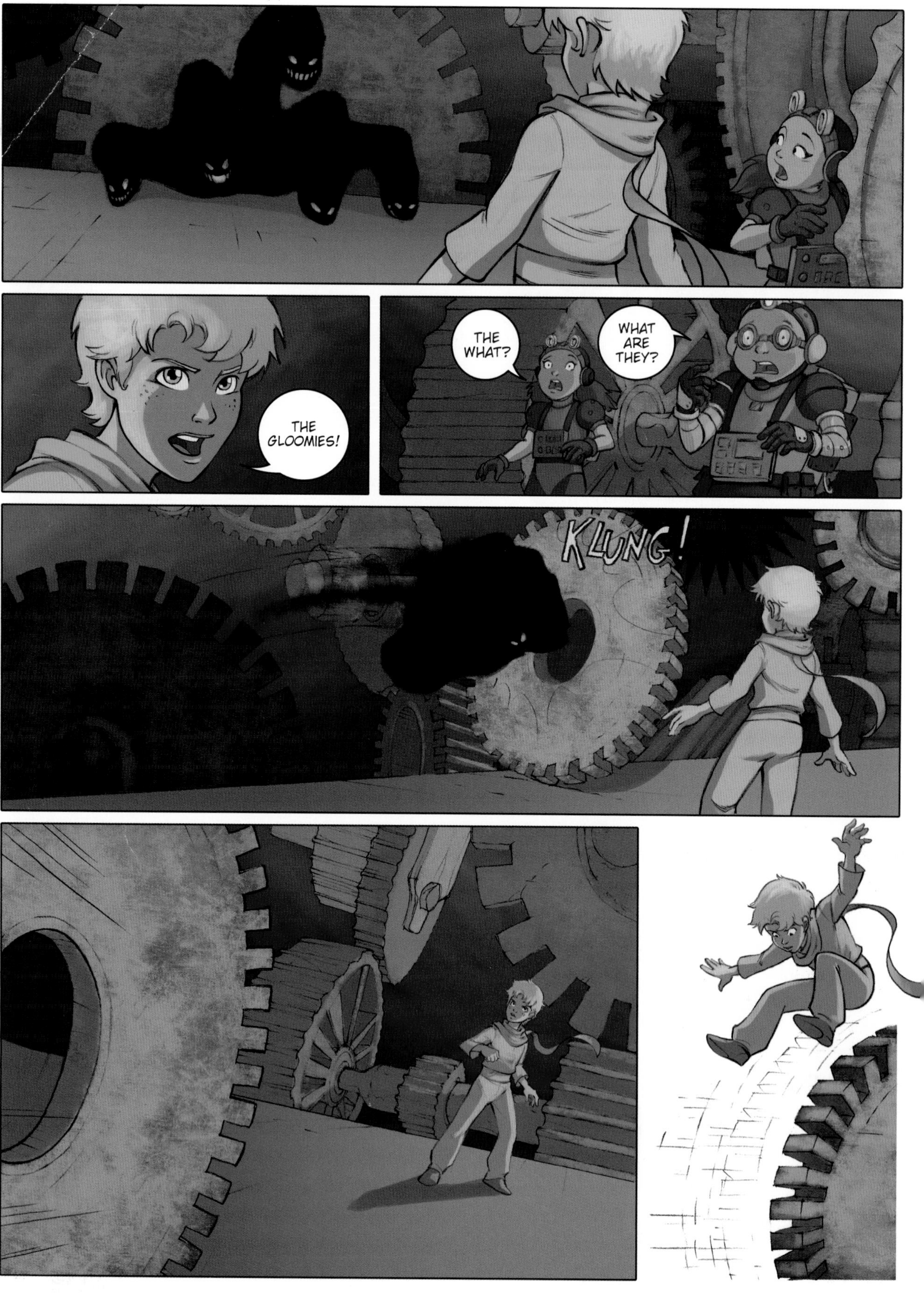
THE GLOOMIES!
THE WHAT?
WHAT ARE THEY?
KLUNG!

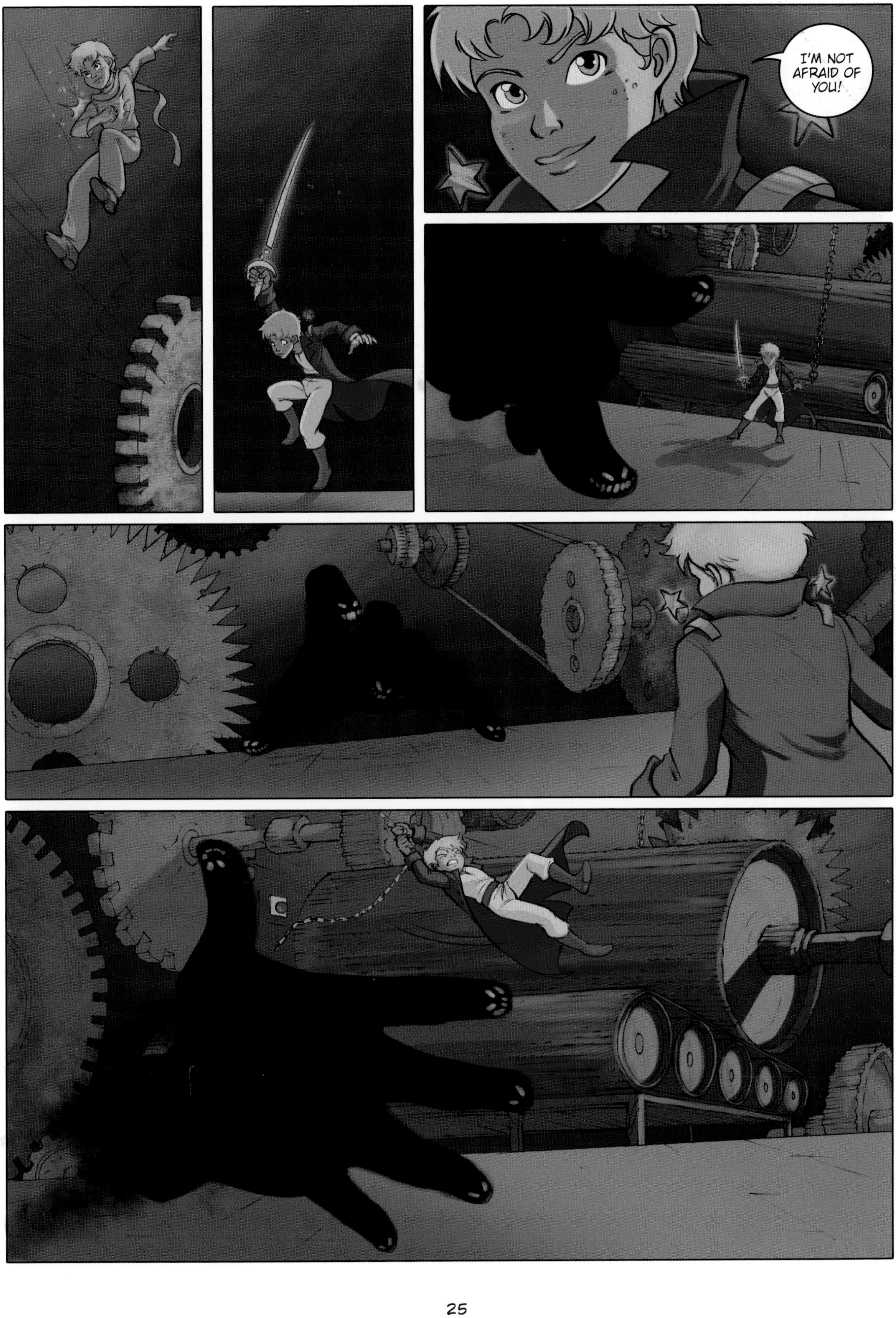
I'M NOT AFRAID OF YOU!

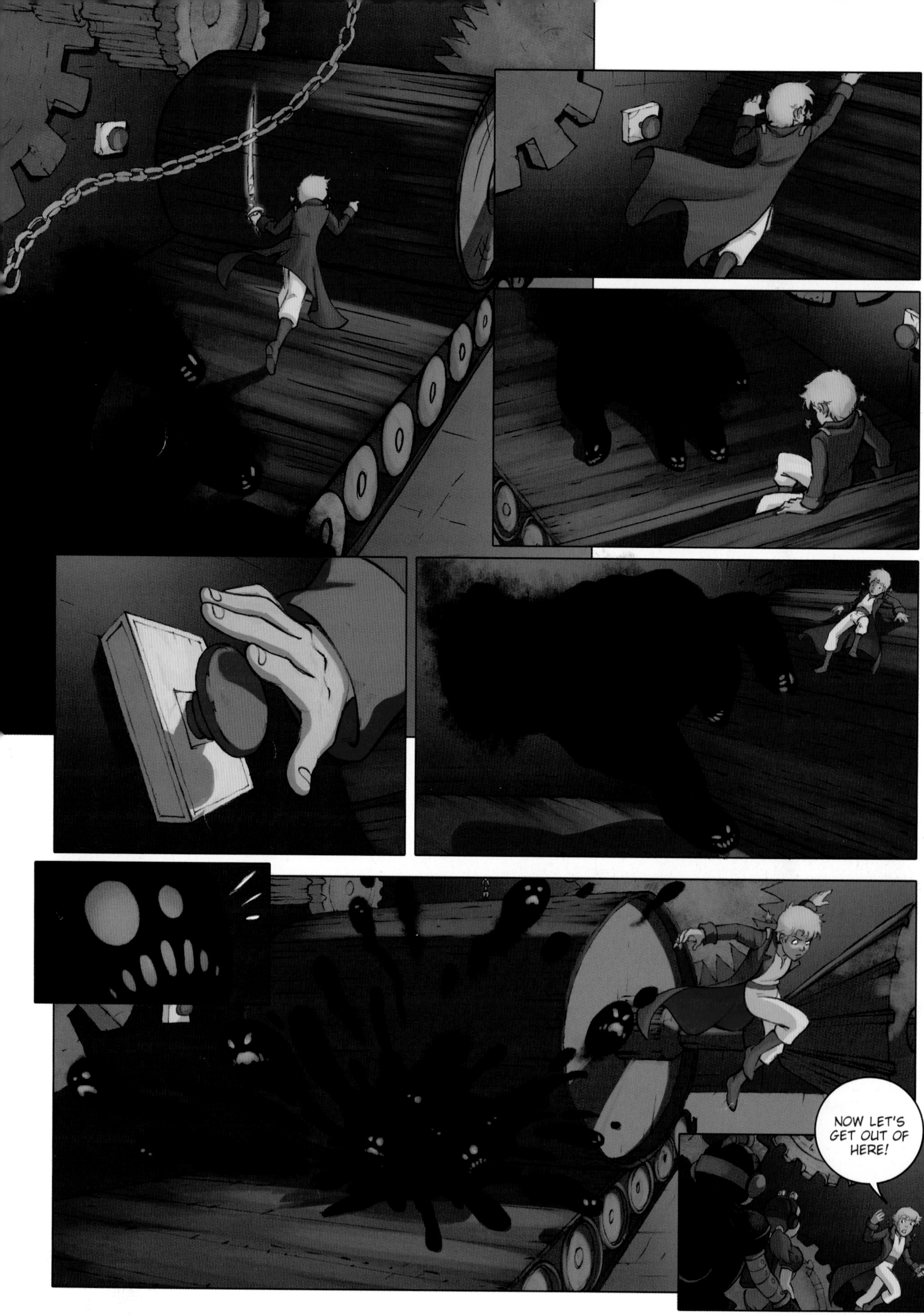
NOW LET'S GET OUT OF HERE!

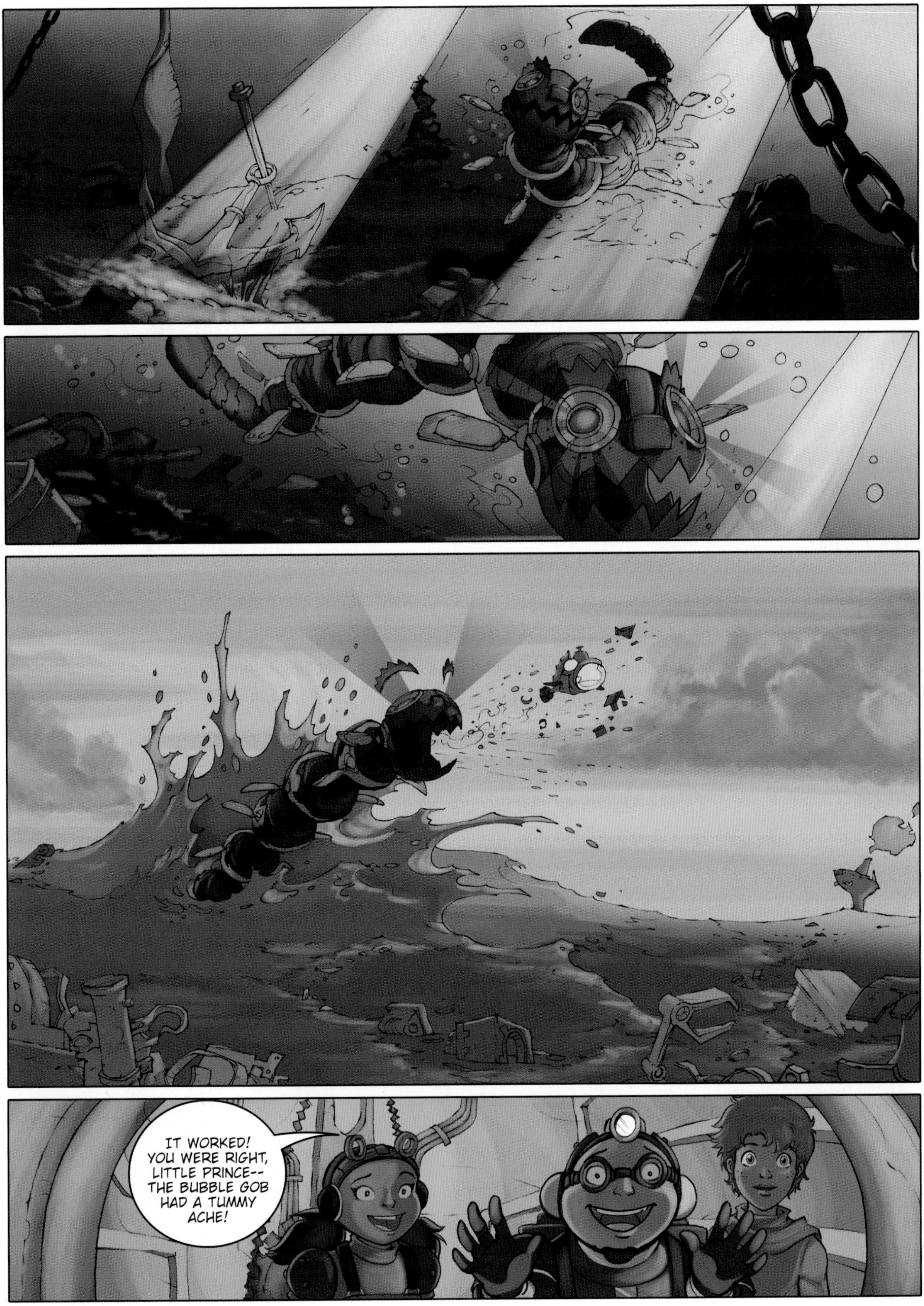
IT WORKED! YOU WERE RIGHT, LITTLE PRINCE-- THE BUBBLE GOB HAD A TUMMY ACHE!

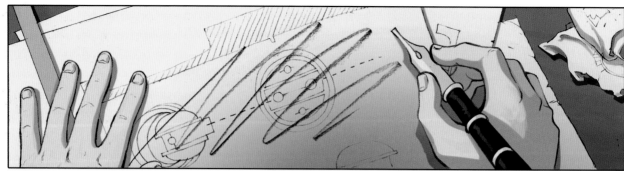

NO, NO, NO! IT WON'T WORK!

THERE'S NO SOLUTION!

HAVE A LITTLE PATIENCE...

...AFTER ALL, THE PROBLEM IS QUITE COMPLICATED... HSSS...

I KEEP HEARING STRANGE SOUNDS! SOMETHING'S TERRIBLY WRONG-- I KNOW IT!

DON'T WORRY. IT'S ONLY SSSOME SSSILLY INVENTIONS DISSSCARDED BY YOUR FRIENDS.

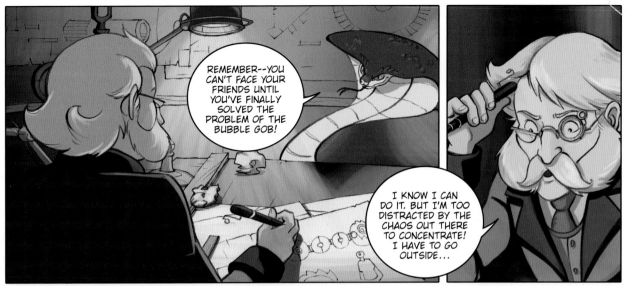

REMEMBER--YOU CAN'T FACE YOUR FRIENDS UNTIL YOU'VE FINALLY SOLVED THE PROBLEM OF THE BUBBLE GOB!

I KNOW I CAN DO IT. BUT I'M TOO DISTRACTED BY THE CHAOS OUT THERE TO CONCENTRATE! I HAVE TO GO OUTSIDE...

...JUST TO CHECK!

ILNIOS CAN TAKE CARE OF THINGS OUT THERE. DON'T YOU TRUST HER?

BESIDES, YOU HAVEN'T SOLVED THE PROBLEM YET. IF YOU LEAVE NOW, EVERYONE WILL LOSE CONFIDENCE IN YOU.

YOU'RE RIGHT. NO ONE MUST SEE ME UNTIL THE PROBLEM HAS BEEN SOLVED!

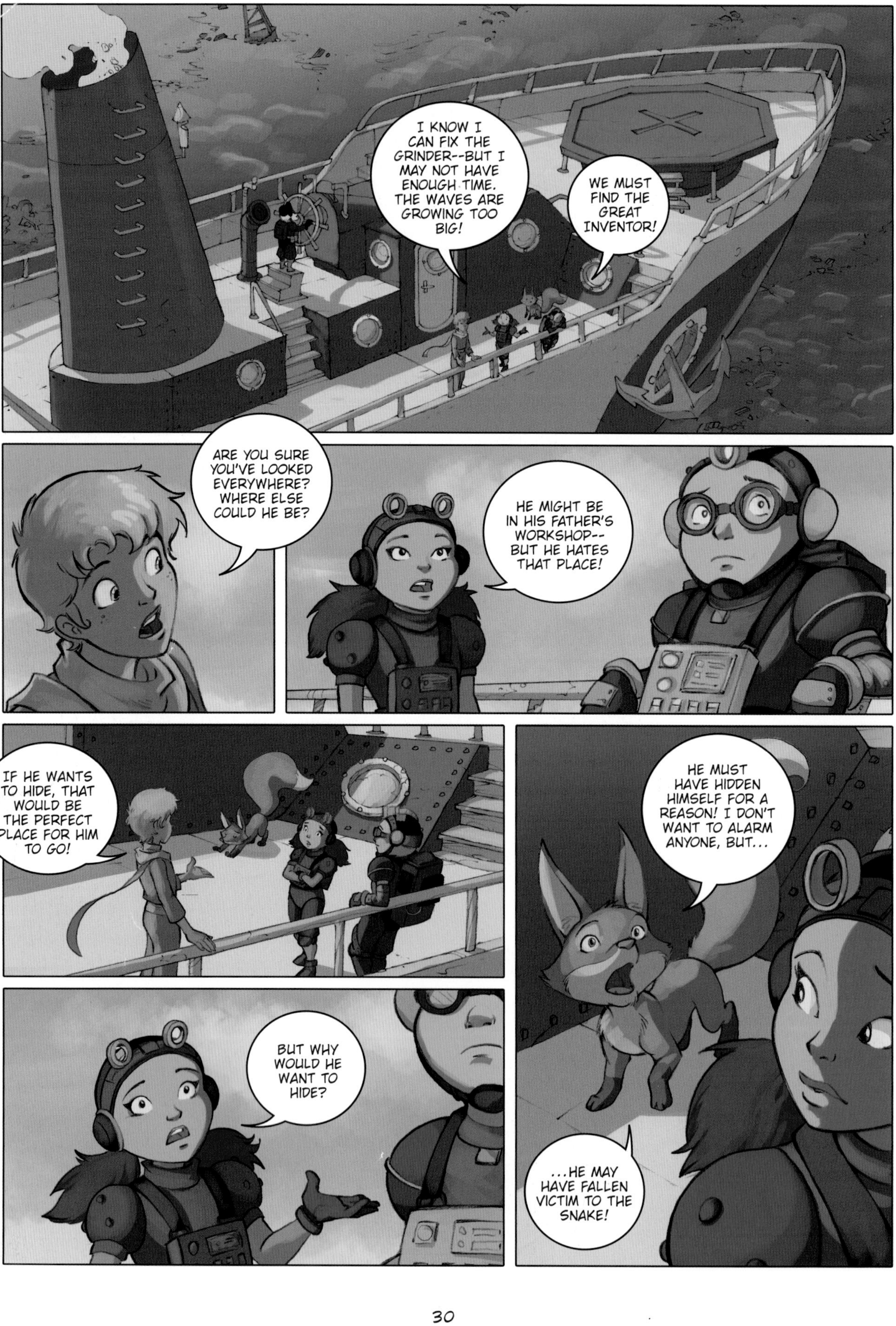
I KNOW I CAN FIX THE GRINDER--BUT I MAY NOT HAVE ENOUGH TIME. THE WAVES ARE GROWING TOO BIG!
WE MUST FIND THE GREAT INVENTOR!
ARE YOU SURE YOU'VE LOOKED EVERYWHERE? WHERE ELSE COULD HE BE?
HE MIGHT BE IN HIS FATHER'S WORKSHOP-- BUT HE HATES THAT PLACE!
IF HE WANTS TO HIDE, THAT WOULD BE THE PERFECT PLACE FOR HIM TO GO!
HE MUST HAVE HIDDEN HIMSELF FOR A REASON! I DON'T WANT TO ALARM ANYONE, BUT...
BUT WHY WOULD HE WANT TO HIDE?
...HE MAY HAVE FALLEN VICTIM TO THE SNAKE!

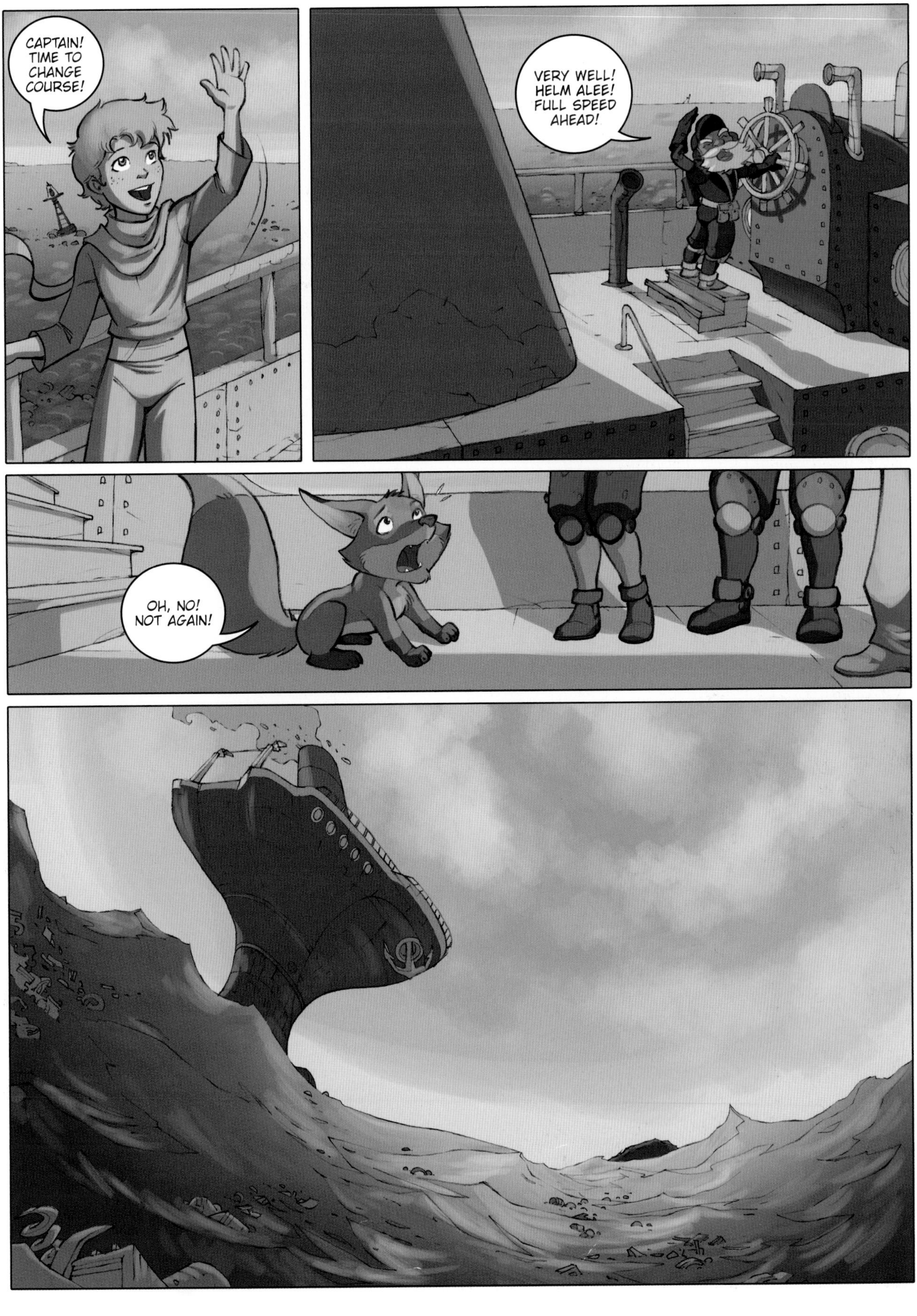
CAPTAIN! TIME TO CHANGE COURSE!
VERY WELL! HELM ALEE! FULL SPEED AHEAD!
OH, NO! NOT AGAIN!

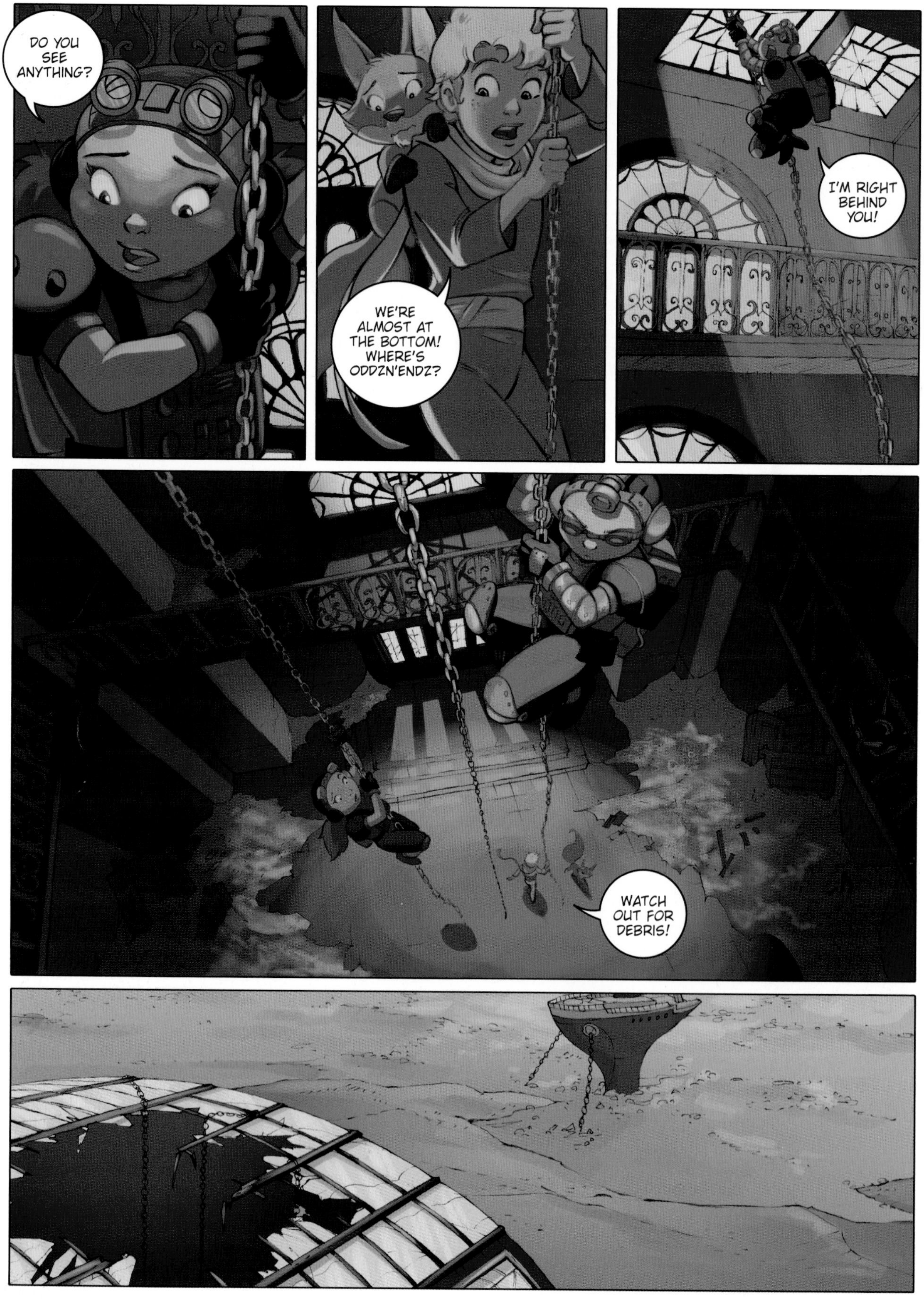
DO YOU SEE ANYTHING?
WE'RE ALMOST AT THE BOTTOM! WHERE'S ODDZN'ENDZ?
I'M RIGHT BEHIND YOU!
WATCH OUT FOR DEBRIS!

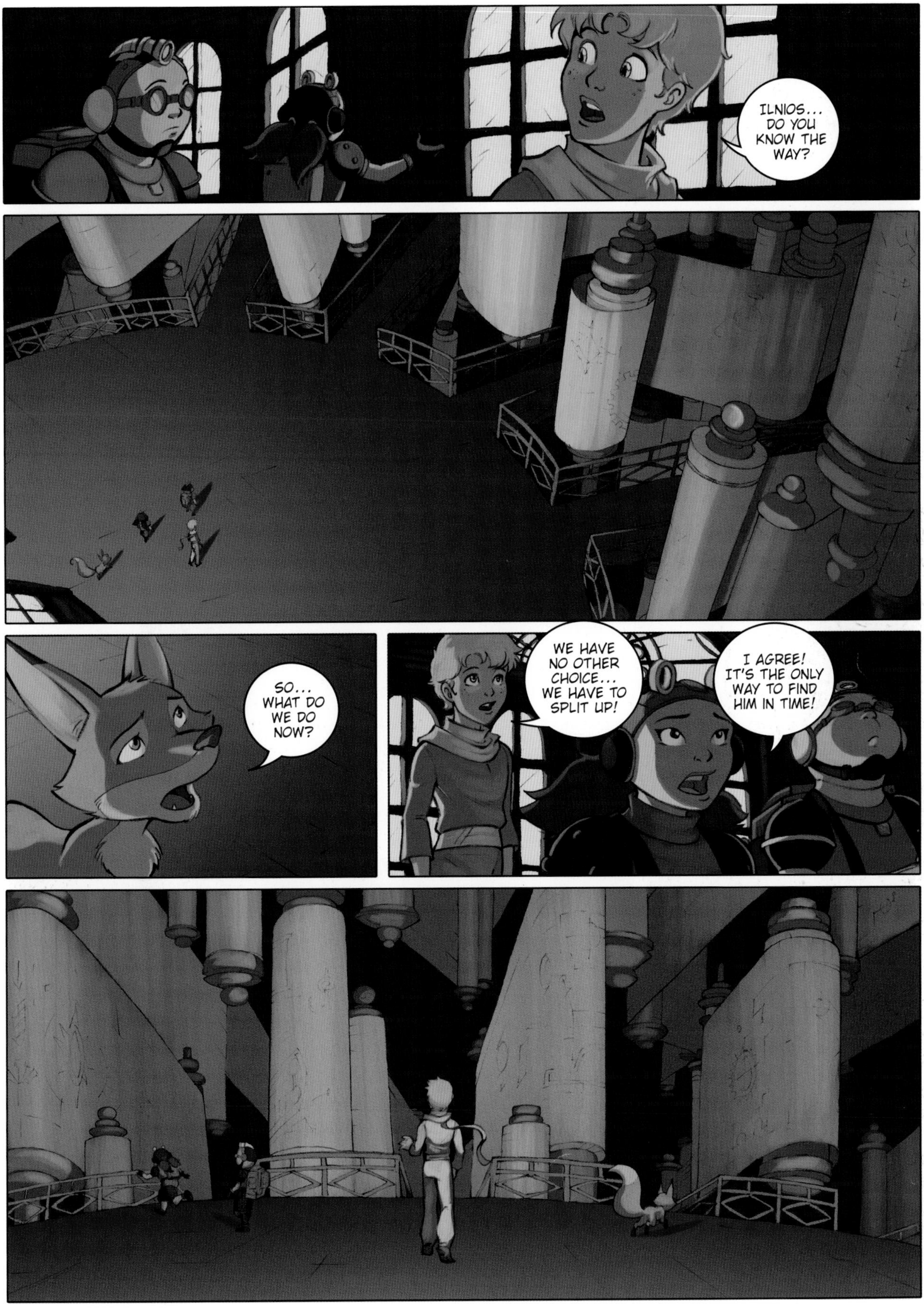
ILNIOS... DO YOU KNOW THE WAY?
SO... WHAT DO WE DO NOW?
WE HAVE NO OTHER CHOICE... WE HAVE TO SPLIT UP!
I AGREE! IT'S THE ONLY WAY TO FIND HIM IN TIME!

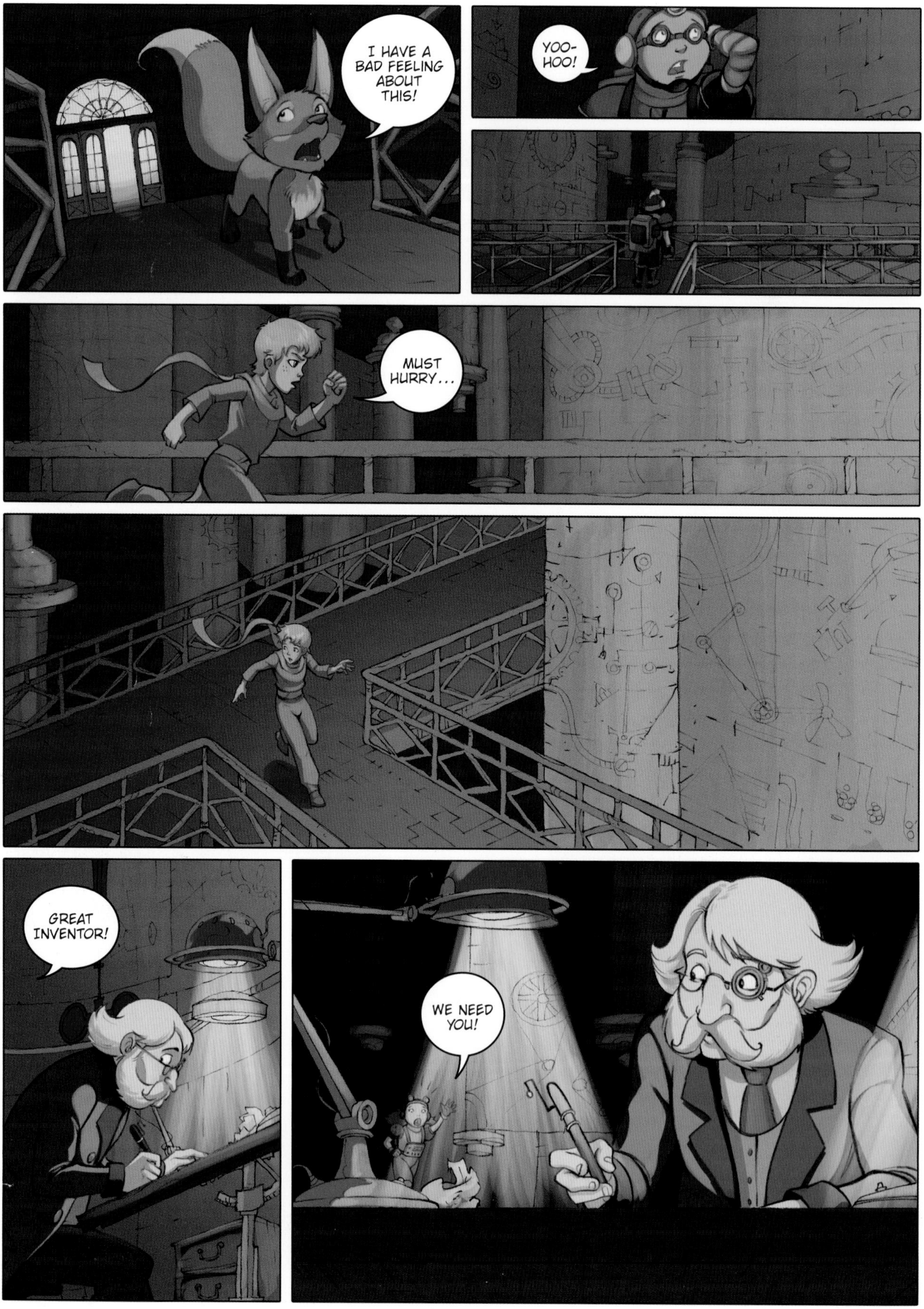
I HAVE A BAD FEELING ABOUT THIS!
YOO-HOO!
MUST HURRY...
GREAT INVENTOR!
WE NEED YOU!

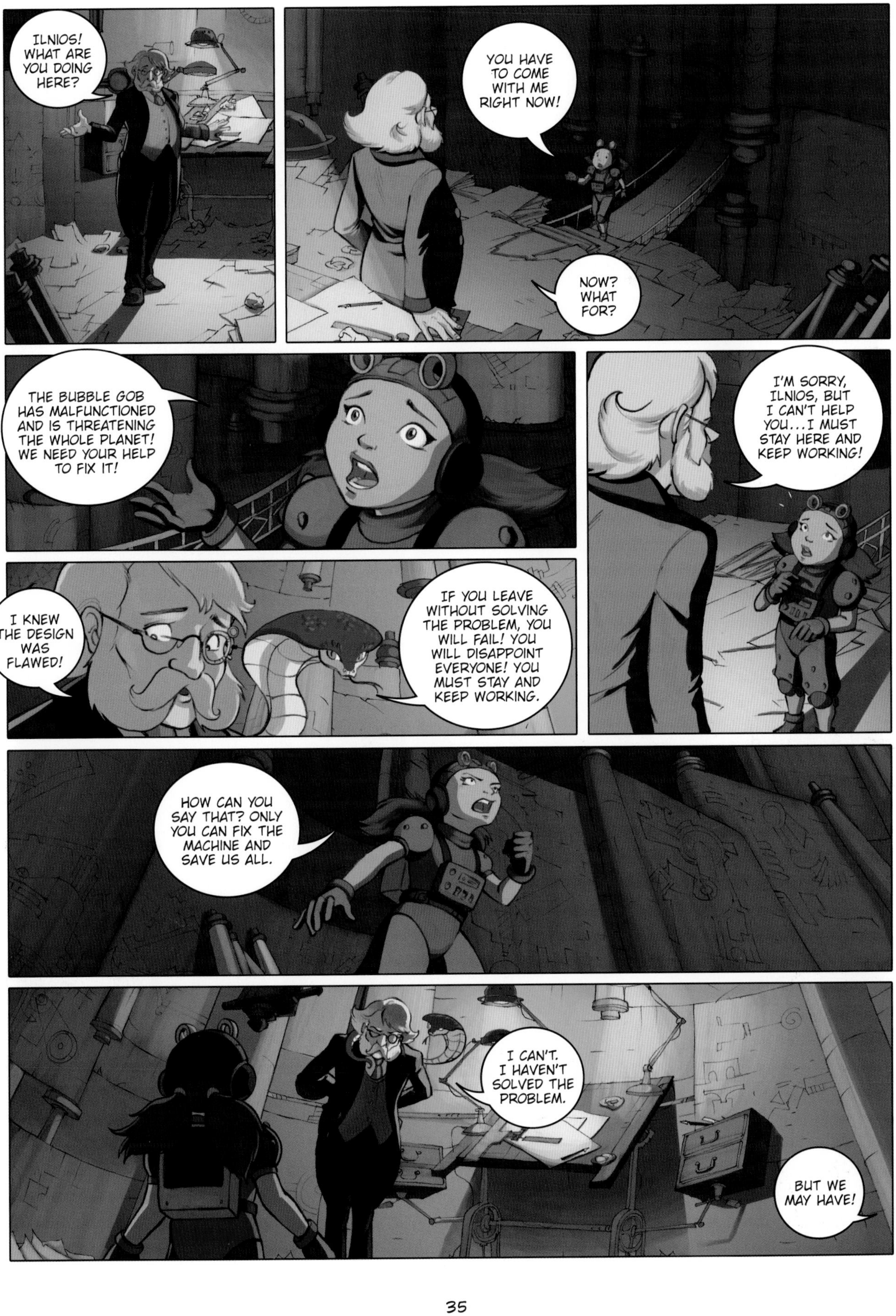
ILNIOS! WHAT ARE YOU DOING HERE?
YOU HAVE TO COME WITH ME RIGHT NOW!
NOW? WHAT FOR?
THE BUBBLE GOB HAS MALFUNCTIONED AND IS THREATENING THE WHOLE PLANET! WE NEED YOUR HELP TO FIX IT!
I KNEW THE DESIGN WAS FLAWED!
IF YOU LEAVE WITHOUT SOLVING THE PROBLEM, YOU WILL FAIL! YOU WILL DISAPPOINT EVERYONE! YOU MUST STAY AND KEEP WORKING.
I'M SORRY, ILNIOS, BUT I CAN'T HELP YOU... I MUST STAY HERE AND KEEP WORKING!
HOW CAN YOU SAY THAT? ONLY YOU CAN FIX THE MACHINE AND SAVE US ALL.
I CAN'T. I HAVEN'T SOLVED THE PROBLEM.
BUT WE MAY HAVE!

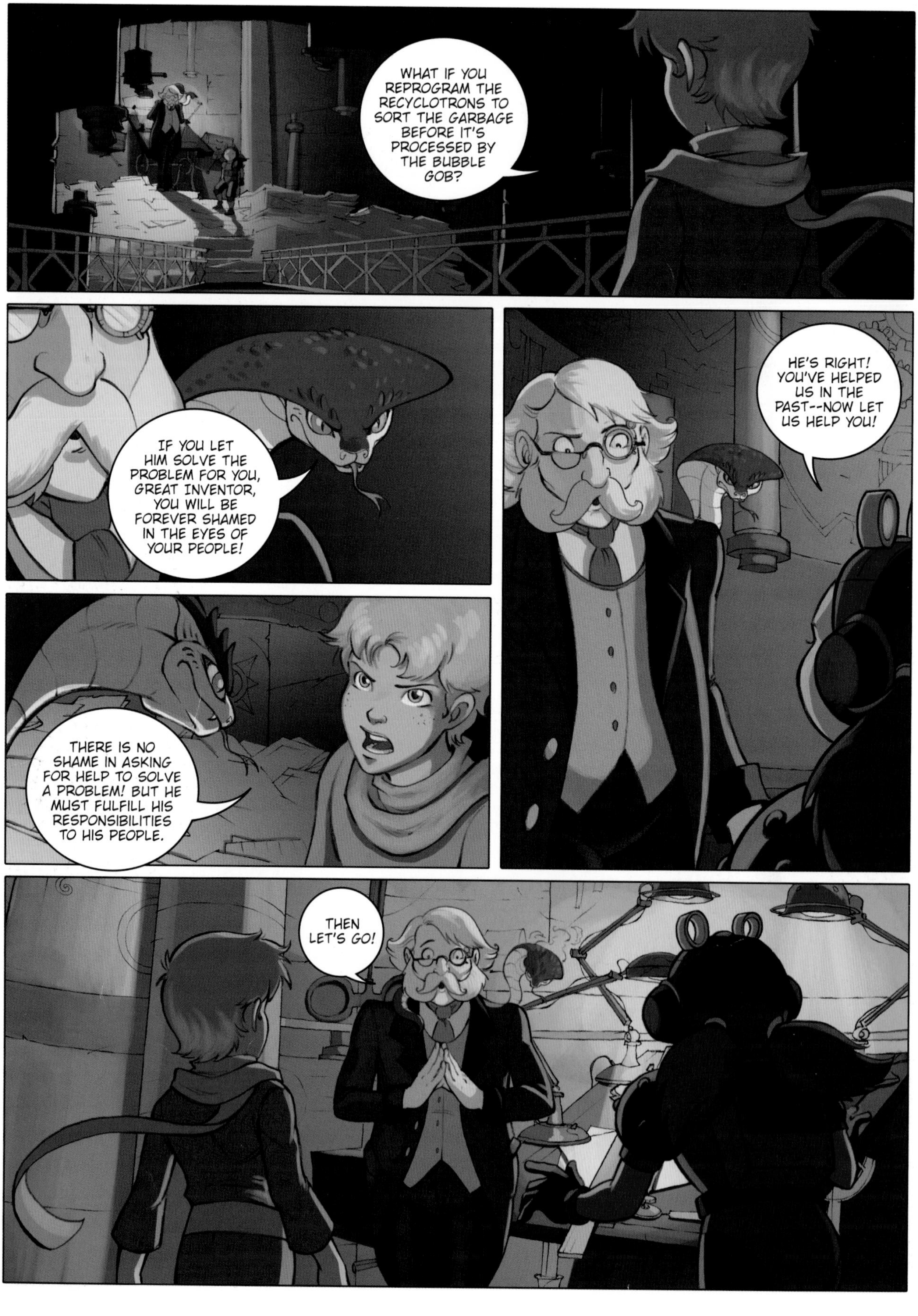
WHAT IF YOU REPROGRAM THE RECYCLOTRONS TO SORT THE GARBAGE BEFORE IT'S PROCESSED BY THE BUBBLE GOB?
IF YOU LET HIM SOLVE THE PROBLEM FOR YOU, GREAT INVENTOR, YOU WILL BE FOREVER SHAMED IN THE EYES OF YOUR PEOPLE!
THERE IS NO SHAME IN ASKING FOR HELP TO SOLVE A PROBLEM! BUT HE MUST FULFILL HIS RESPONSIBILITIES TO HIS PEOPLE.
HE'S RIGHT! YOU'VE HELPED US IN THE PAST--NOW LET US HELP YOU!
THEN LET'S GO!

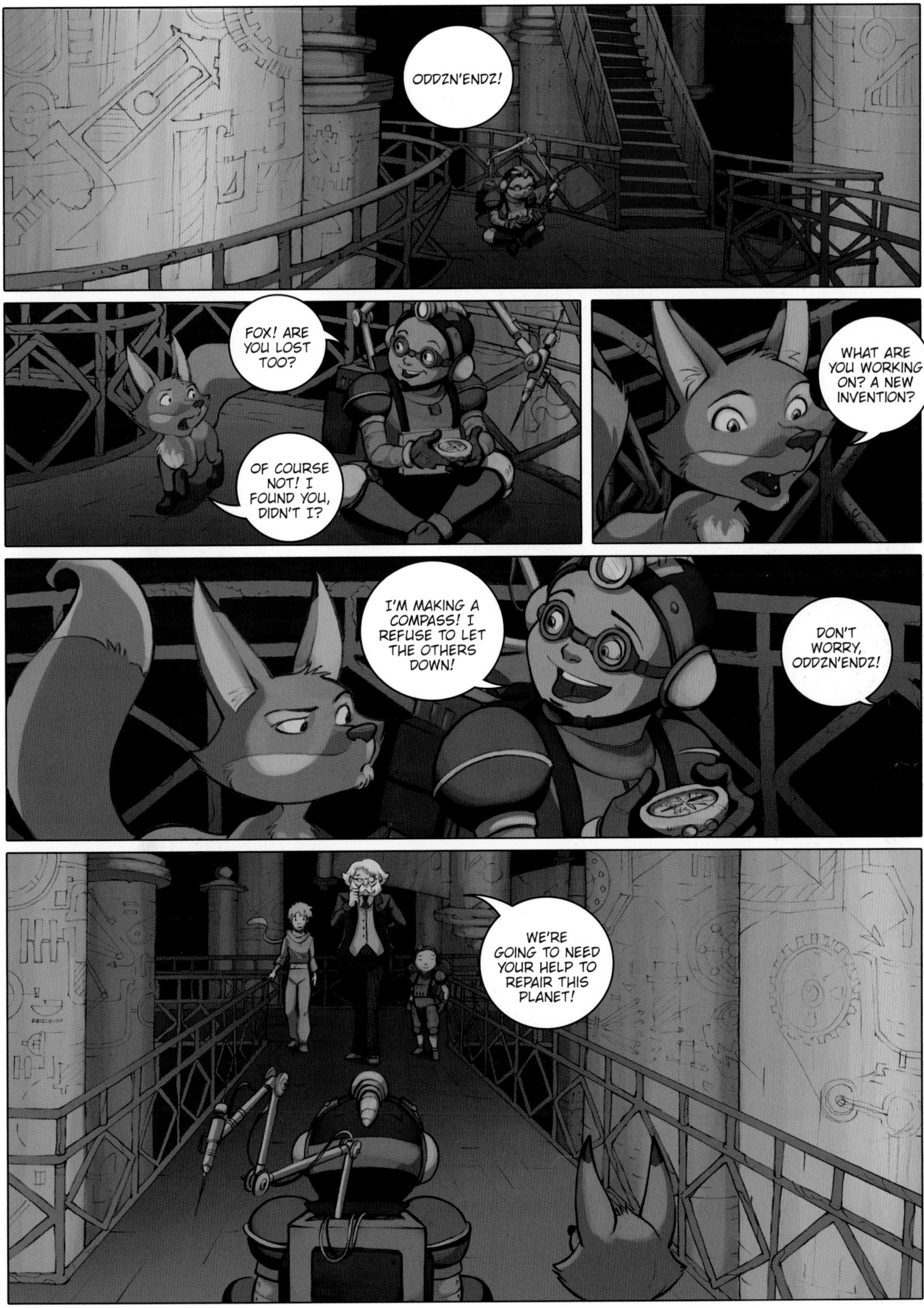
ODDZN'ENDZ!
FOX! ARE YOU LOST TOO?
OF COURSE NOT! I FOUND YOU, DIDN'T I?
WHAT ARE YOU WORKING ON? A NEW INVENTION?
I'M MAKING A COMPASS! I REFUSE TO LET THE OTHERS DOWN!
DON'T WORRY, ODDZN'ENDZ!
WE'RE GOING TO NEED YOUR HELP TO REPAIR THIS PLANET!

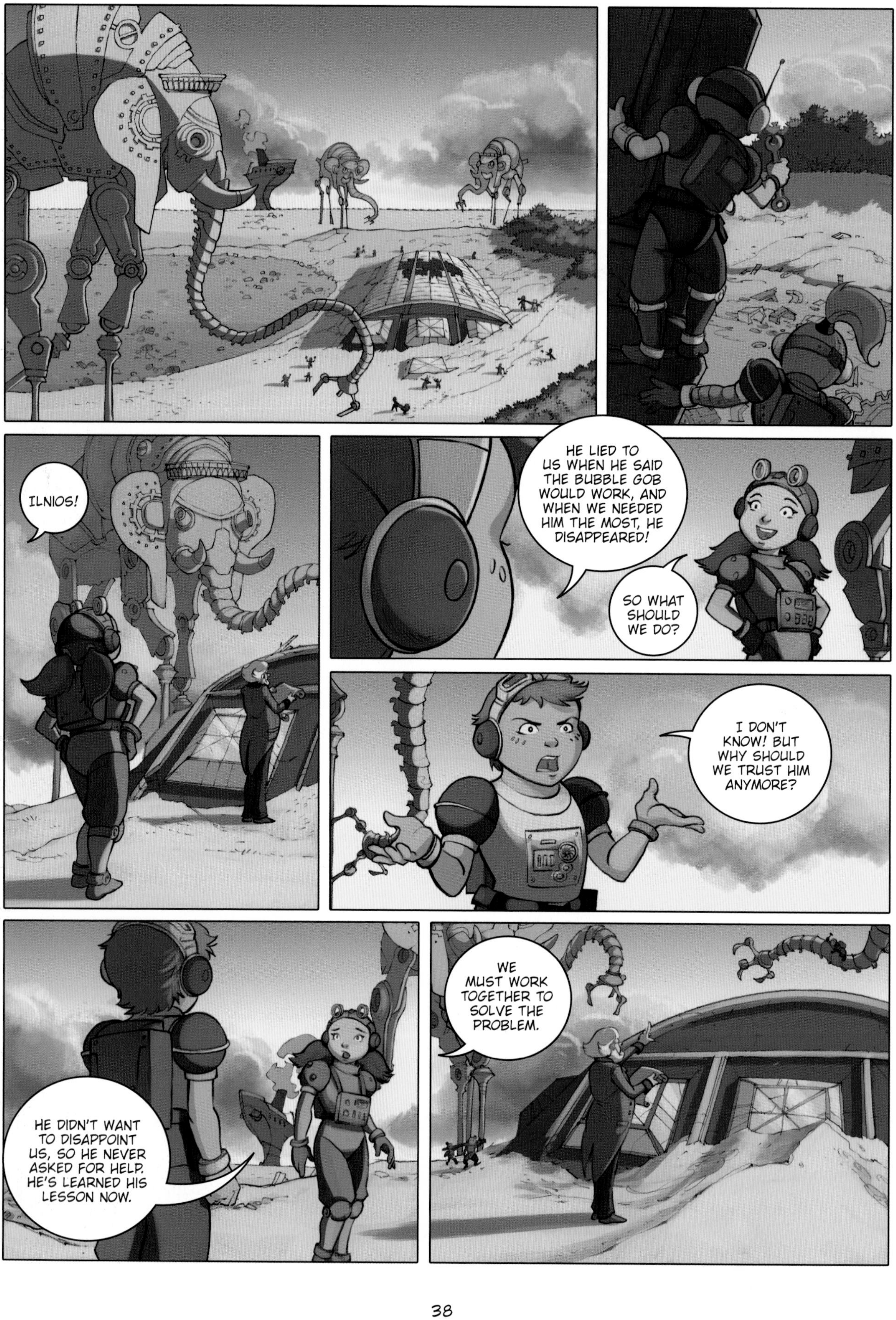
ILNIOS!
HE LIED TO US WHEN HE SAID THE BUBBLE GOB WOULD WORK, AND WHEN WE NEEDED HIM THE MOST, HE DISAPPEARED!
SO WHAT SHOULD WE DO?
I DON'T KNOW! BUT WHY SHOULD WE TRUST HIM ANYMORE?
HE DIDN'T WANT TO DISAPPOINT US, SO HE NEVER ASKED FOR HELP. HE'S LEARNED HIS LESSON NOW.
WE MUST WORK TOGETHER TO SOLVE THE PROBLEM.

SO, GREAT INVENTOR, HAVE YOU FINISHED THE DESIGN?

I'M ALMOST DONE! BUT WE DON'T HAVE ENOUGH NUTS AND BOLTS!

NUTS AND BOLTS? ARE YOU KIDDING?

EVERYTHING WE NEED, WE CAN GET FROM THE TRASH!

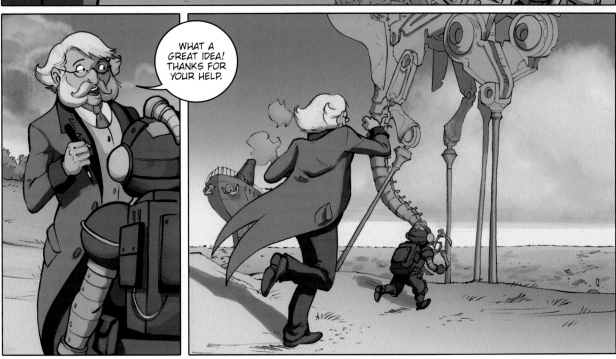

WHAT A GREAT IDEA! THANKS FOR YOUR HELP.

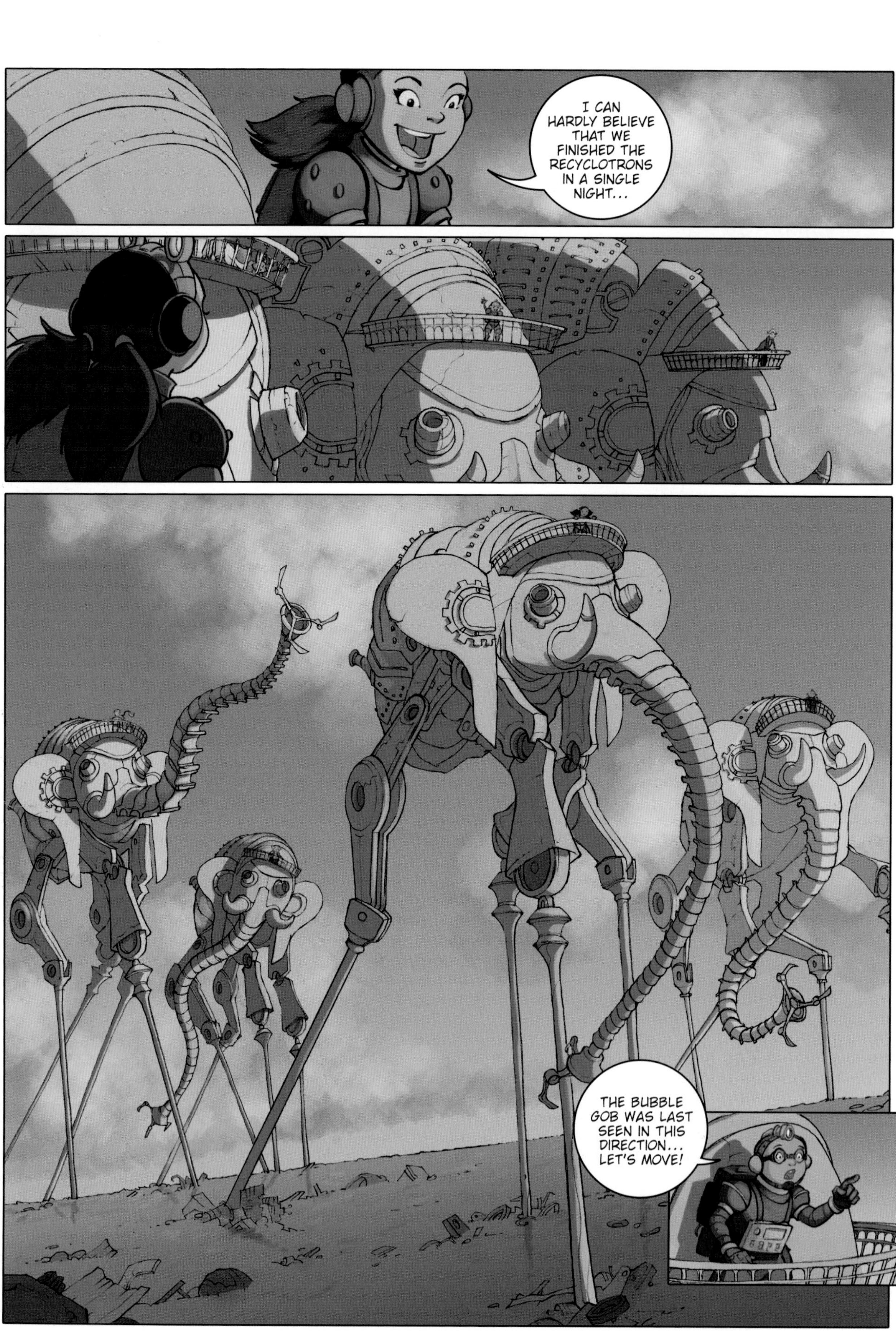
I CAN HARDLY BELIEVE THAT WE FINISHED THE RECYCLOTRONS IN A SINGLE NIGHT...
THE BUBBLE GOB WAS LAST SEEN IN THIS DIRECTION... LET'S MOVE!

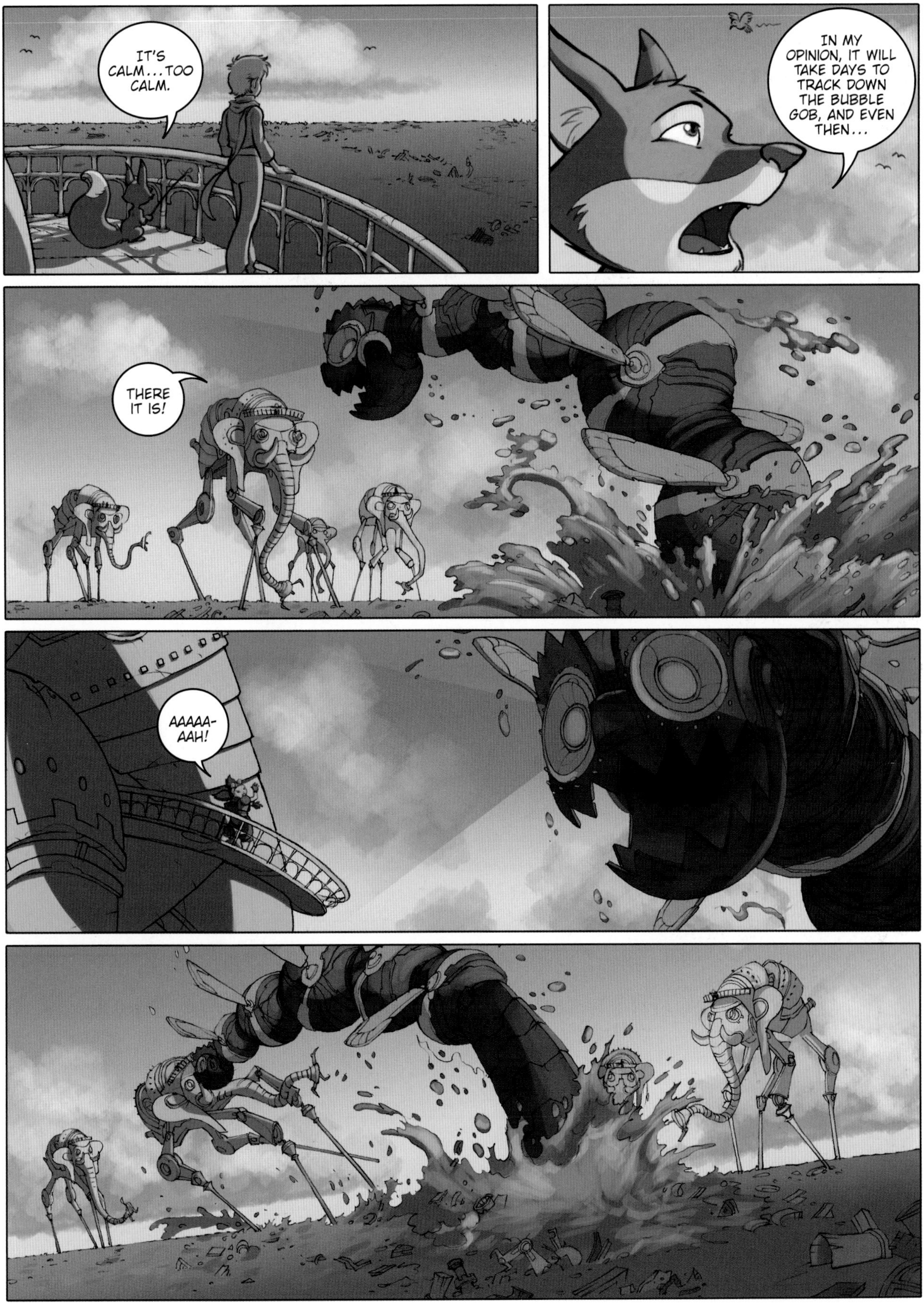
IT'S CALM...TOO CALM.
IN MY OPINION, IT WILL TAKE DAYS TO TRACK DOWN THE BUBBLE GOB, AND EVEN THEN...
THERE IT IS!
AAAAA-AAH!

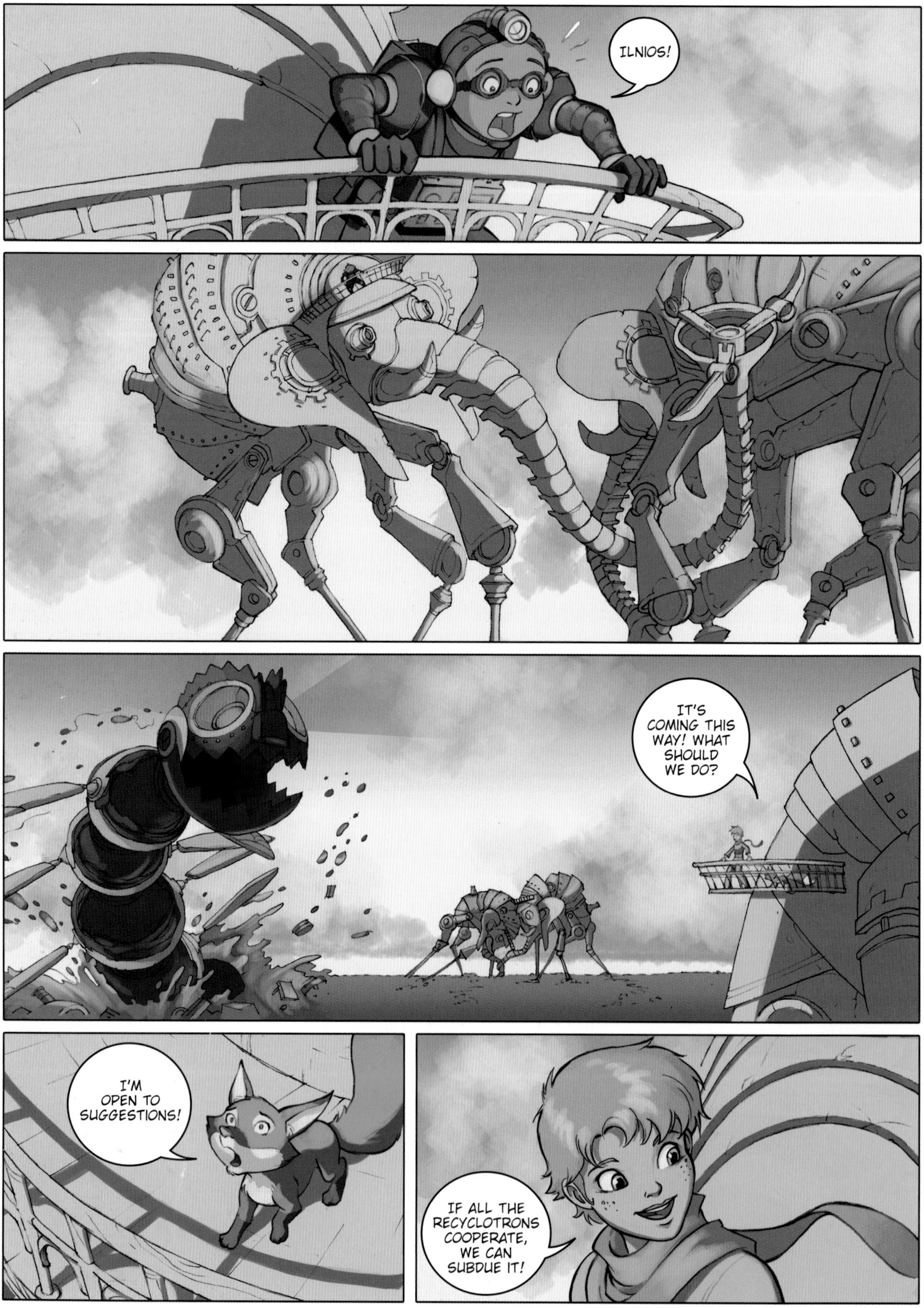
ILNIOS!
IT'S COMING THIS WAY! WHAT SHOULD WE DO?
I'M OPEN TO SUGGESTIONS!
IF ALL THE RECYCLOTRONS COOPERATE, WE CAN SUBDUE IT!

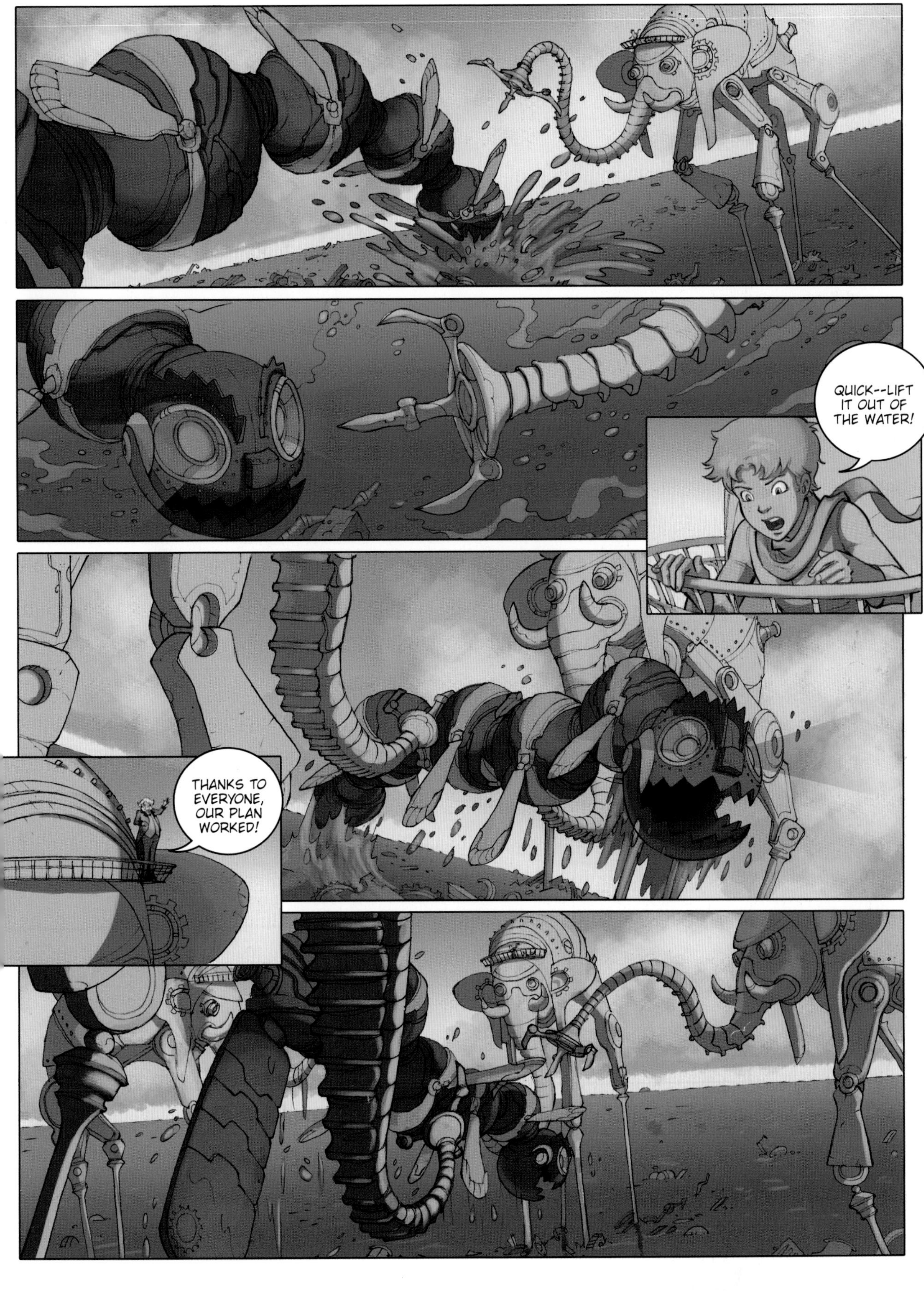
QUICK--LIFT IT OUT OF THE WATER!
THANKS TO EVERYONE, OUR PLAN WORKED!

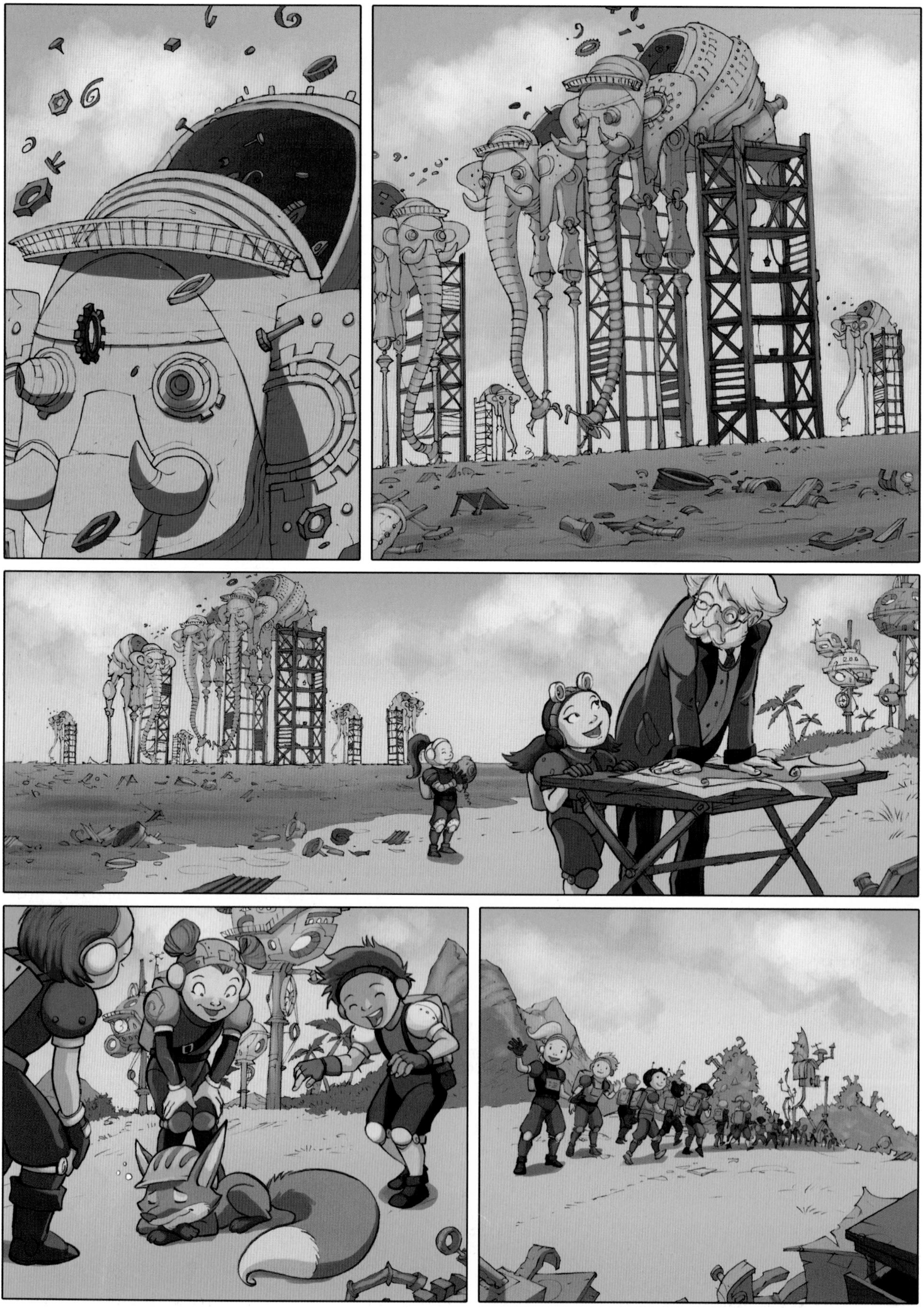

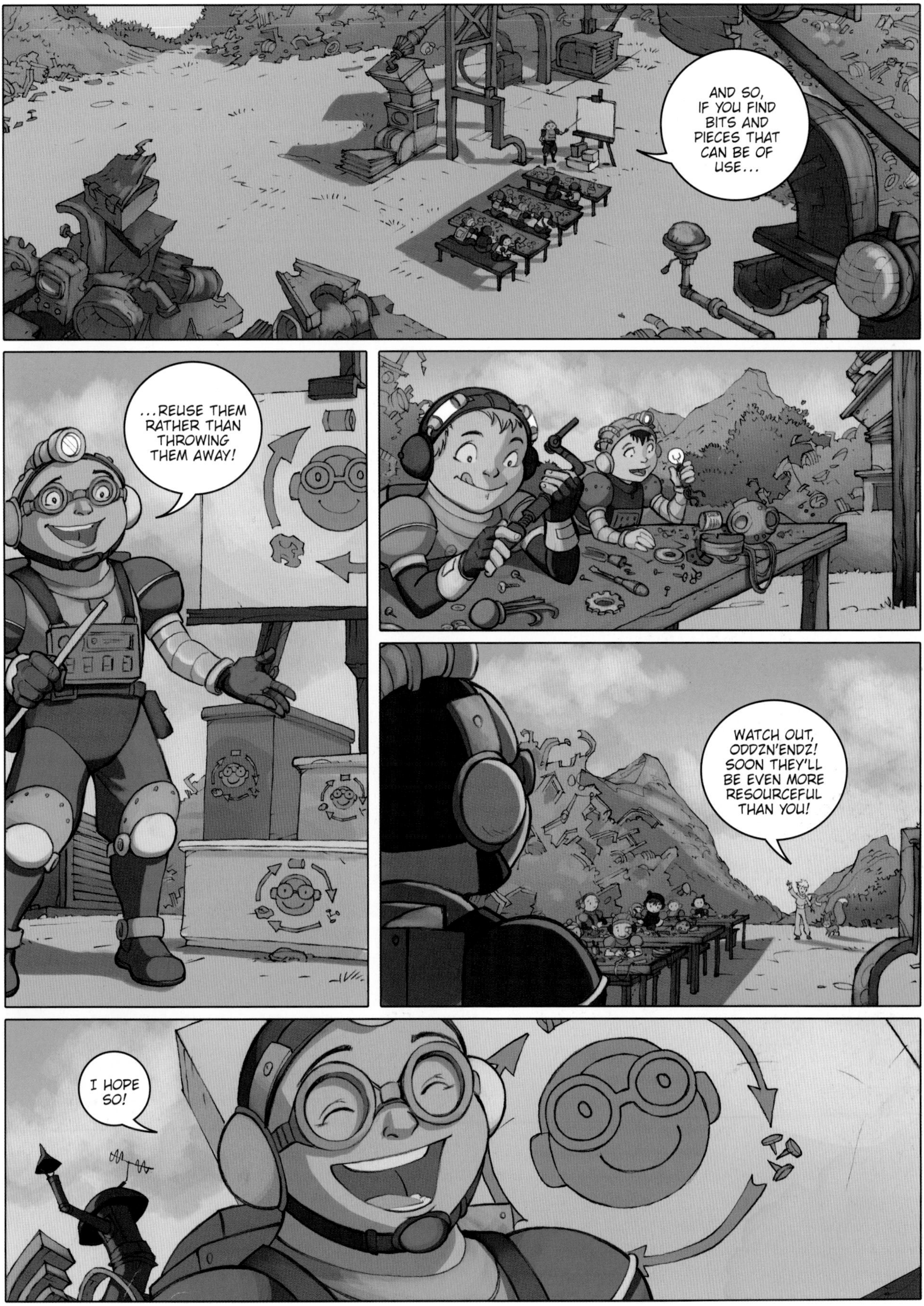
AND SO, IF YOU FIND BITS AND PIECES THAT CAN BE OF USE...
...REUSE THEM RATHER THAN THROWING THEM AWAY!
WATCH OUT, ODDZN'ENDZ! SOON THEY'LL BE EVEN MORE RESOURCEFUL THAN YOU!
I HOPE SO!

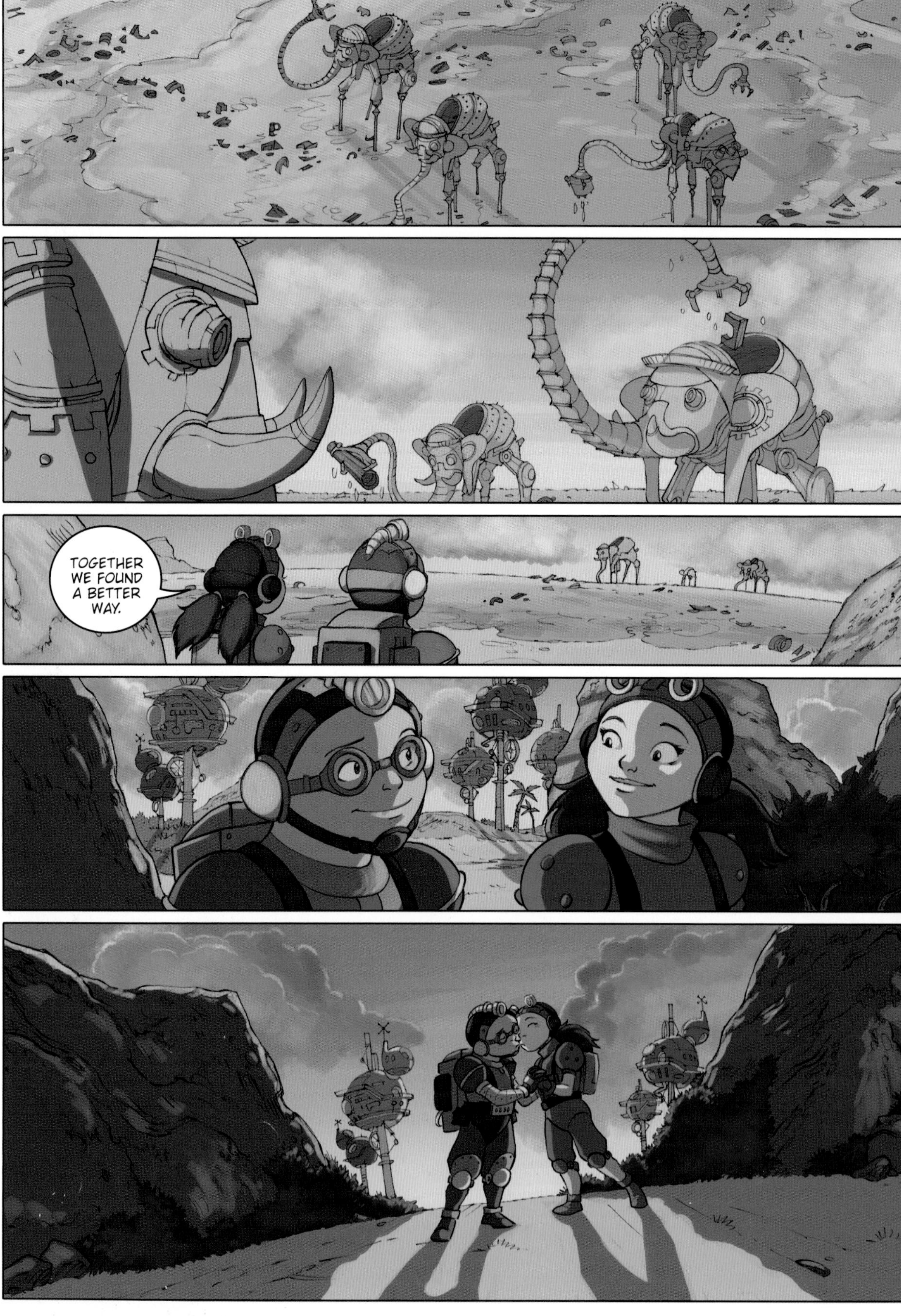
TOGETHER WE FOUND A BETTER WAY.

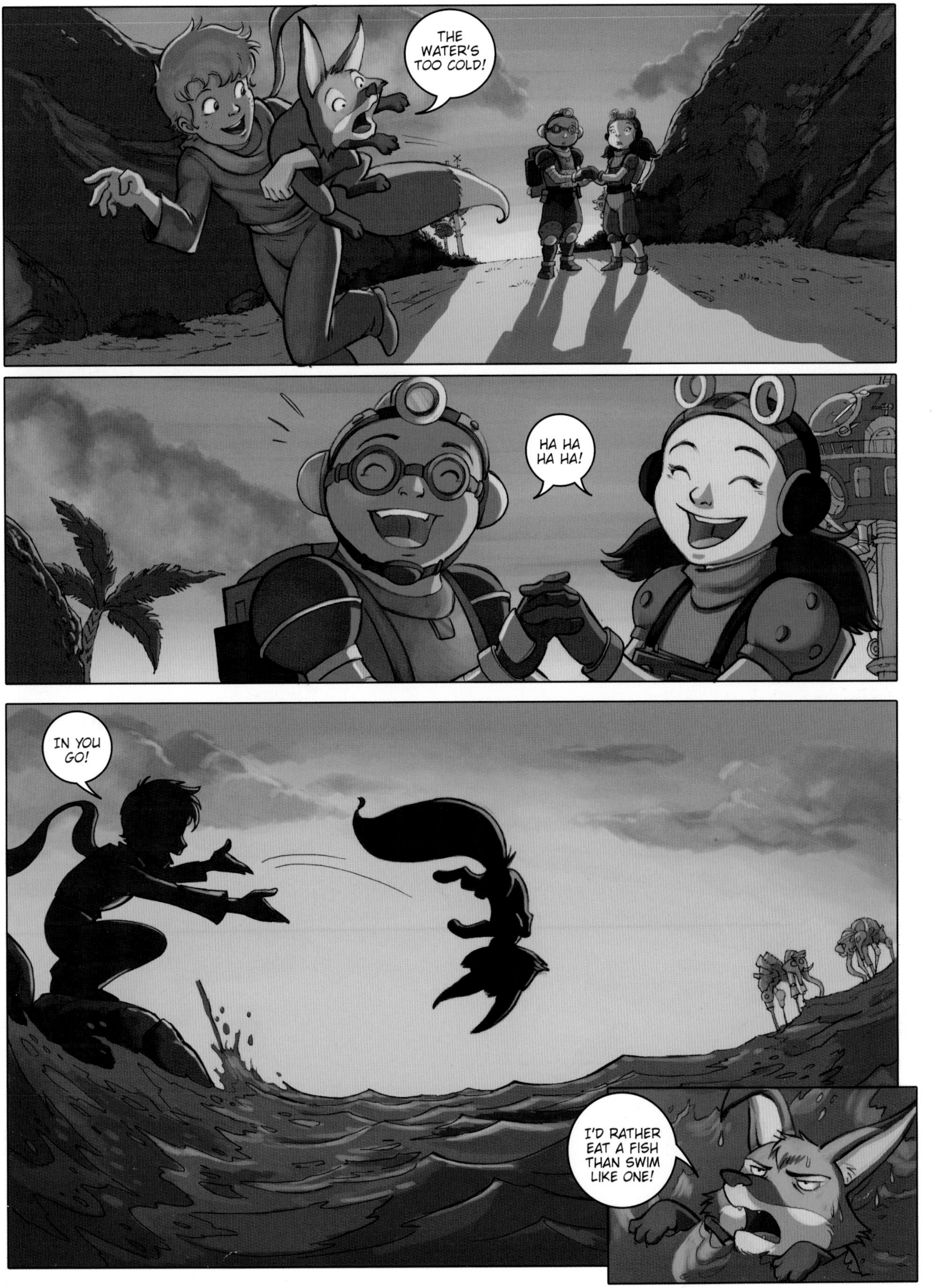
THE WATER'S TOO COLD!
HA HA HA HA!
IN YOU GO!
I'D RATHER EAT A FISH THAN SWIM LIKE ONE!

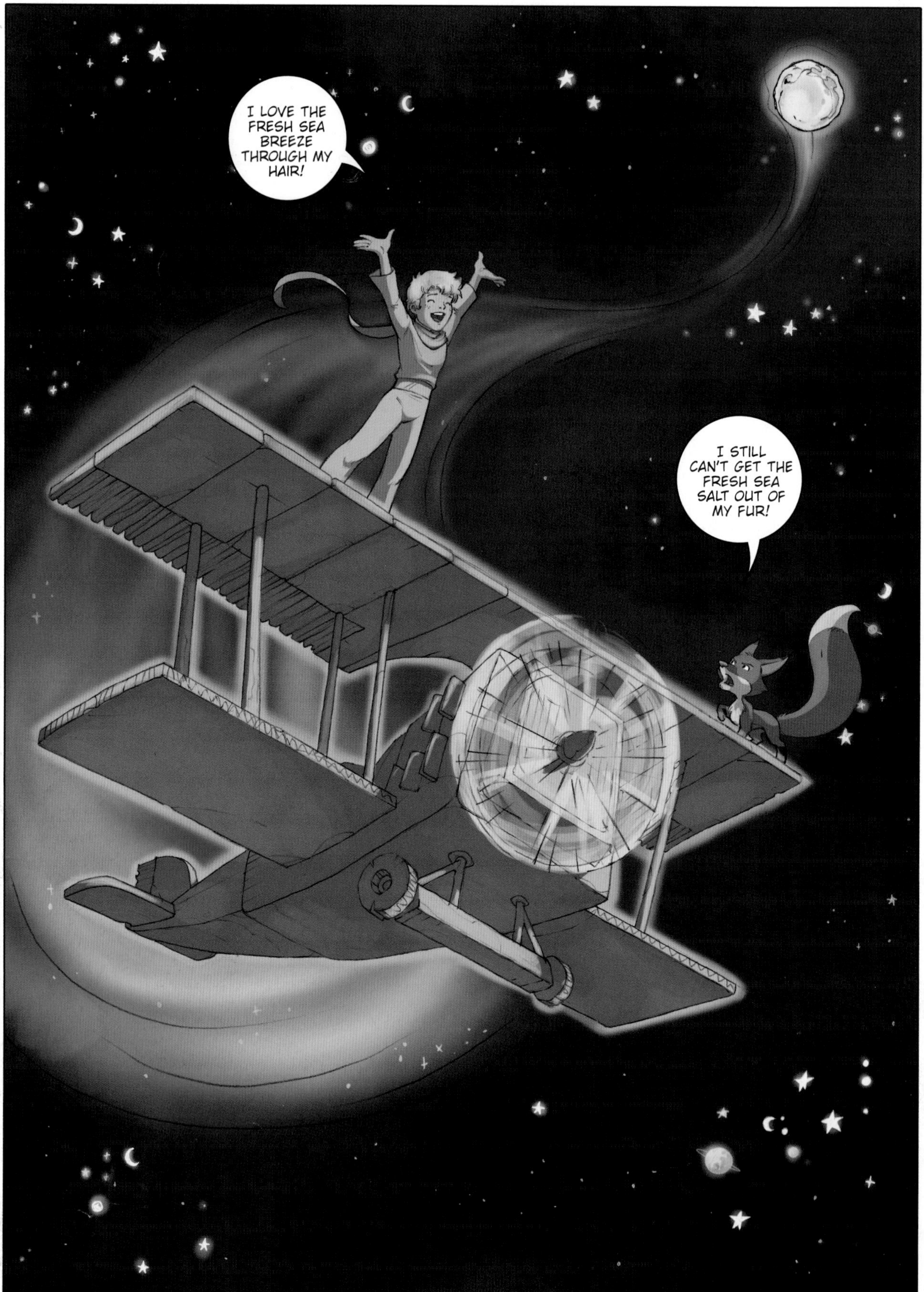
I LOVE THE FRESH SEA BREEZE THROUGH MY HAIR!
I STILL CAN'T GET THE FRESH SEA SALT OUT OF MY FUR!

Read all the Books in *The Little Prince* series

Book 1: The Planet of Wind

Book 2: The Planet of the Firebird

Book 3: The Planet of Music

Book 4: The Planet of Jade

Book 5: The Star Snatcher's Planet

Book 6: The Planet of the Night Globes

Book 7: The Planet of the Overhearers

Book 8: The Planet of the Tortoise Driver

Book 9 : The Planet of the Giant

Book 10 : The Planet of Trainiacs

Book 11 : The Planet of Libris

Book 12 : The Planet of Ludokaa

Book 13 : The Planet of Tear-Eaters

Book 14 : The Planet of the Grand Buffoon

Book 15 : The Planet of the Gargand

Book 16 : The Planet of Gehom

Book 17 : The Planet of the Bubble Gob

Book 18 : The Planet of Time

Book 19 : The Planet of the Cublix

Book 20 : The Planet of Coppelius

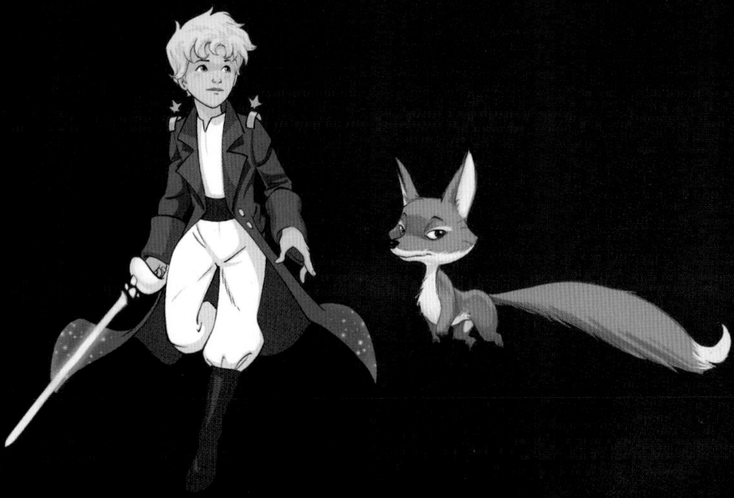

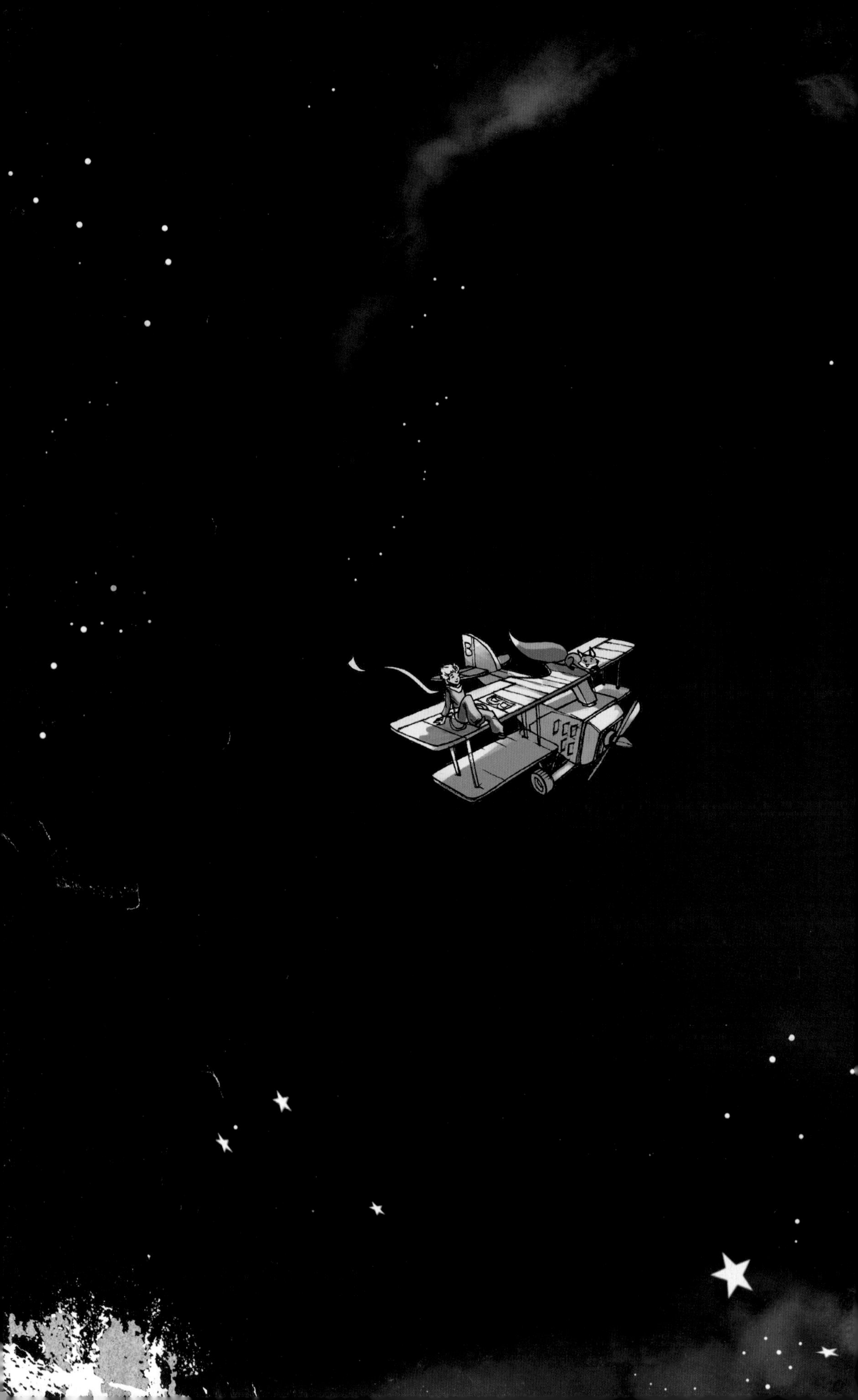
B

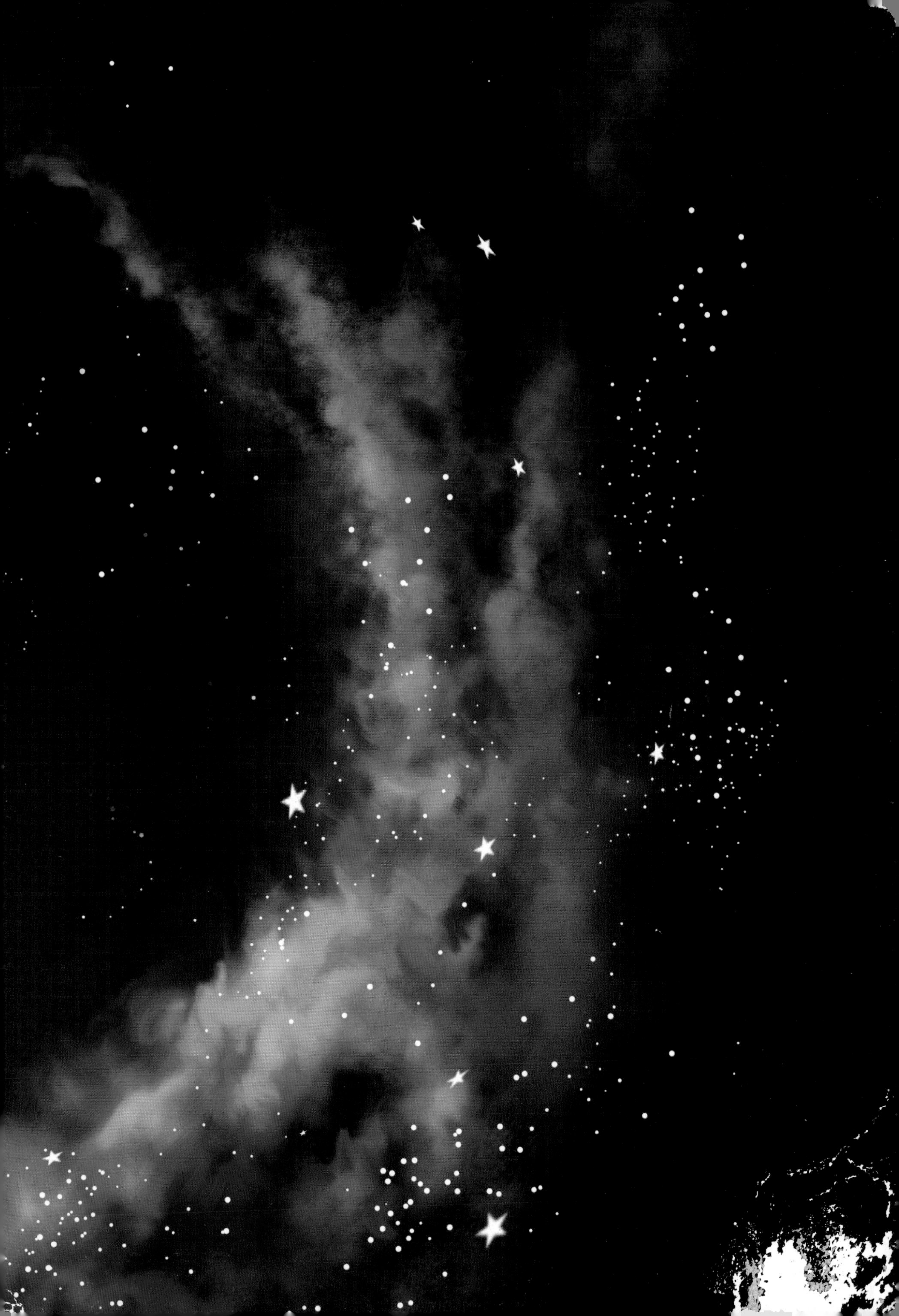